"Jam-Jam, I'v .em," I whispered into the phone.

Realistically I knew Ash probably couldn't hear me from downstairs; nonetheless, this was a top secret call, and I wasn't taking any chances.

"Everything okay? Say 'Pizza with extra olives' if you're being held against your will," Jamie whispered back. He was mocking me, but little did he know I was about to blow his ginger mind.

"I-think-I'm-in-love-with-Ash," I spat out as one word.

DREAMSPUN DESIRES

Dear Reader,

Love is the dream. It dazzles us, makes us stronger, and brings us to our knees. Dreamspun Desires tell stories of love featuring your favorite heartwarming heroes, captivating plots, and exotic locations. Stories that make your breath catch and your imagination soar.

In the pages of these wonderful love stories, readers can escape to a world where love conquers all, the tenderness of a first kiss sweeps you away, and your heart pounds at the sight of the one you love.

When you put it all together, you find romance in its truest form.

Love always finds a way.

Elizabeth North

Executive Director
Dreamspinner Press

Veronica Cochrane

RHYTHM OF US

DREAMSPUN DESIRES

PUBLISHED BY

DREAMSPINNER
PRESS

Published by
DREAMSPINNER PRESS

5032 Capital Circle SW, Suite 2, PMB# 279,
Tallahassee, FL 32305-7886 USA
www.dreamspinnerpress.com

This is a work of fiction. Names, characters, places, and incidents either are the product of author imagination or are used fictitiously, and any resemblance to actual persons, living or dead, business establishments, events, or locales is entirely coincidental.

Rhythm of Us
© 2022 Veronica Cochrane

Cover Art
© 2022 L.C. Chase
http://www.lcchase.com

Cover content is for illustrative purposes only and any person depicted on the cover is a model.

Paperback ISBN 978-1-64108-403-1
Digital ISBN: 978-1-64108-402-4
Paperback published July 2022
v. 1.0

Printed in the United States of America

VERONICA COCHRANE is a contemporary m/m romance author. She enjoys all things creative, including going to live performances, writing, and—most recently—crochet! As an avid reader and lifelong romantic, Veronica loves seeing characters fall in love, overcome realistic obstacles, and find their happily ever after. Veronica lives in Ontario, Canada, with her husband.

Website: veronicacochrane.com
Twitter: @veronicacwrites
Email: veronicacochrane@outlook.com

By Veronica Cochrane

DREAMSPUN DESIRES
Inevitable Duets
Next to Me
Dance with Me
Rhythm of Us

Published by **DREAMSPINNER PRESS**
www.dreamspinnerpress.com

Acknowledgments

ALL of the Inevitable Duets books feature artistic partnerships that guide and strengthen the band's music. Art is inherently collaborative and—like the Thorns—I am so lucky to have amazing people helping these stories become the best version of what's in my head. Thank you to my husband, my friends and family, everyone at Dreamspinner Press, and to all the readers for supporting the Thorns's journey.

Author's Note

THIS was not the story I set out to write.

Throughout the Inevitable Duets series, Dean Phillips somehow went from a side character whom we see a handful of times to an increasingly large presence in the Thorns world. After I wrote the first chapter of what was supposed to be solely Ash's story, it was obvious Dean wasn't going to miss his opportunity to finally capture center stage.

Or let Ash end up with anyone but him.

The chemistry Dean and Ash had been building throughout the series came through in the first pages and grew naturally. It was impossible to resist or deny their connection. So I just kept writing and let the characters guide my words, trusting their humor and their hearts.

This is the story Ash and Dean wanted to tell, and it couldn't be a better way to culminate the Inevitable Thorns saga.

With love,
Veronica

Ash

I FLOPPED on my bed, utterly exhausted. It felt like years since I'd been home and at least months since I'd gotten a decent night's rest. Touring with my band, the Inevitable Thorns, throughout Europe for the past eight months had been beyond a dream come true. But nobody warned me it would also be fucking draining.

Brrinnng. Brrinnng.

I groaned into the pillow, not wanting to deal with whoever was on the other end of my phone. After a few more rings, it mercifully went quiet, and I breathed a sigh of relief. My eyes fluttered shut as my body melted into the comfortable mattress.

Brrinnng. Brrinnng.

Bloody fucking hell.

There couldn't possibly be anything in the world that was as urgent in this moment as getting some damn sleep. My phone kept ringing with an offensively perky chime. I fished it out of my pocket and glanced at the name on the screen before rolling my eyes and silencing it, knowing that wouldn't do me any good. He would just keep calling back.

I tossed my phone next to me on the cool white blanket, waiting for the predictable ringing to start again.

Dingdong. Diiiingdong.

Looking at my phone through bleary eyes, it took me a second to recognize that this time the sound wasn't coming from the handheld device. No, the doorbell was far and away the greater of the two evils.

Dingdong. Dingdong. Dingdong. Diiiingdong.

I was going to kill him. Flat out fucking dig-a-hole-in-the-backyard murder him.

The door chimed over and over as my phone started ringing again. I puffed out a sigh of resignation. As much as I knew I would regret it, I left the decadent luxury of my sheets to go take care of the last thing in the world I wanted to deal with right now. After plodding down the hall in my bare feet, I ran my fingers along the smooth handrail and descended the stairs. My steps were slow and heavy, my muscles still loosening up from being cramped in an airplane for the better part of fourteen hours.

I unlatched the door, mentally bracing myself for the energy of the bright almost-summer sunlight and the unwanted visitor.

The ringing and dinging stopped immediately as the smiling face of my best friend and bandmate, Dean Phillips, came into view. He brushed his dark-chocolate ringlet curls from his eyes, needing a trim after months on the road. His leather jacket, black skinny jeans, and moto boots looked far too hot for this weather. Not that what he wore surprised me. It was exactly the same outfit he'd had on the last time I'd seen him, when we parted ways at the airport. Less than two hours ago.

"Oh good, you're home," Dean said casually, as if he hadn't been blowing up my phone and doorbell for the past ten minutes.

He invited himself in, walked past me in the entryway, and went through to the kitchen. I stared at the conspicuously large suitcase Dean left on my stoop.

"Why yes, Dean, please come in," I muttered to myself.

I dragged the suitcase inside before closing and locking the door to keep the warm air out. Dean and I had grown up together, or at least in proximity to each other, I supposed. The tiny town of Amberwood, Massachusetts, was barely a pinprick on a map. Not even worthy of having its own high school. When we outgrew the local elementary, the kids in our community were bused off to a neighboring town where the sizable military base generated a substantial enough populace to merit a secondary school. That's where Dean and I first really became acquainted, on the school bus. I remember seeing Dean around when I was young—it was hard not to notice anyone in a town with only a couple hundred permanent residents—but our folks never ran in the same circles.

My parents were both string players with the Boston Symphony Orchestra, choosing to deal with the hour-long commute into the city several times a week in order to live a small-town lifestyle the rest of the time. Both their families had grown up in the community, and although moving probably would have made sense, it was never a priority for them. From the time I was young, I remember spending many nights with various family members when my parents were out late performing. That was of course in addition to being shuffled to piano lessons, art classes, and tennis practice after school. My parents were far from wealthy or pretentious, but they prioritized giving me as many opportunities as possible so I could figure out what I was passionate about, like they were about orchestral music.

While I kept a practical apartment in New York for when we were recording or doing other business, Amberwood was where I was most at home. I had this four-bedroom house custom built on a large parcel of land about eighteen months ago; however, due to the crazy schedule we kept, I had barely spent any time here so far. Fortunately the band had negotiated at least the next four months off, so I would finally get to enjoy the slower pace of life in my own home.

I followed Dean into the kitchen, where he had evidently made himself comfortable. He cracked the top off one of the beers he must have grabbed from my fridge and handed me the other. After taking a long pull from the bottle, he hopped up on a barstool.

Taking the beer he offered, I nodded an acknowledgment before putting it directly back into the refrigerator. I could practically feel him rolling his eyes at me while my head was turned.

"So I was thinking," he started nonchalantly, "you're really more of a people person, Ashy."

I shook my head. "No, I'm not."

He kept going without acknowledging my interjection. "You'll be lonely as fuck out here all by yourself. Got nobody around for miles. Plus there's probably bears and mooses and all sorts of scary shit like that." Dean paused to scratch his head thoughtfully.

He certainly better hope the music career worked out, because he wouldn't be making his living through acting anytime soon.

I raised my eyebrow at him skeptically, trying to figure out exactly where he was going with this, terrified to know the answer.

"What's your point, Deano?" I asked, caving.

"No point. Was just thinking it might be better for you to have a roommate for a bit. Wouldn't want you to choke on a ham sandwich and not be able to find a Heimlich buddy."

He took a casual drink of his beer.

"And who would this completely selfless Heimlich-doing-slash-bear-deterring person be, Dean?"

"I mean, you would probably want it to be someone you already know. Maybe someone you've lived with and know you can get along with? A trusted wingman or a fellow rhythm player in your band, perhaps?"

"You want to live with me? Here?" I crossed my arms. The last of the energy drained out of my body.

"What a kind offer, Ashy! That's mighty hospitable of you." Dean grinned wide and held up his beer in a mock toast before taking the last sip from the bottle.

"I wasn't inviting…. I was…. Never mind," I muttered, shaking my head.

He pointed upstairs in the direction of the bedrooms in a silent question before taking a few steps away from me.

"Dean!" I exclaimed with enough volume to get his attention.

He turned around slowly, an innocent smile appearing on his stupidly irresistible face. Our female fans knew Dean and I were the only available, unattached members of the Thorns, but that look was the reason why he always ended up getting so much action with our groupies.

Clearly this was happening whether I wanted it to or not. Dean was my best friend—a fucking handful, but my best friend nonetheless. We lived together in tiny buses and cramped dressing rooms for months on end, and we had somehow managed to survive that. My craved time alone slipped out of my grasp as quickly as it had materialized.

I raised my eyebrow at him again, silently demanding the full, nonbullshit story.

"Mom gave my room to my niece." He shook his head in dramatic indignation.

I choked back a laugh before putting my arm over his shoulders and leading him to the stairs. While I wasn't crazy about the idea, I wasn't cruel enough to turn him away when he needed me.

"I'll show you your room."

Dean

I WOKE up in Ash's very comfortable guest room with a big old smile on my face. Although I loved every second of touring with the guys, this dumb little town would forever be home. Knowing I was doing good for my mom made every exhausting night worth it. Lord knows she worked harder than I ever would.

Despite being a single mom to me and my sisters, Harlow and Maci, she always managed to keep food on the table when we were growing up. Now that I had money, she refused to let me buy her a bigger house because she loved her own so much. She was so damn proud of that little rancher on Glenwood Street with the bright blue front door. Even if the size meant she didn't have a bed for me to sleep in when I showed up on her porch yesterday.

In hindsight, I probably should have let her know I was coming.

I grabbed my phone off the nightstand and checked the time: 11:17 a.m. Being home even made me an early riser. I stretched beneath the blue cotton sheets before scratching my balls and doing a quick pit check. Could probably skip a shower today. I threw the covers off, eager to get down to the diner and wander through town this afternoon. See what I had missed in the four months since I had been home at Christmas.

When I opened the door, I almost tripped over my suitcase in the hall. Papa Ash must have left it there for me; he was always looking out for me when I couldn't seem to get my shit together. I backtracked and got dressed. Look at me not walking around his house naked. Already I was being a considerate roommate.

"Hey," Ash greeted me as I approached him in the kitchen.

"Morning," I said. "You been up for a while?"

"Nah, just half an hour or so. Felt like I could sleep for a month. Everything cool in the guest room?"

"Yup, thanks again for letting me crash. Sheets were silky smooth against the goods."

"Oh God. I really don't want to hear about your naked ass touching anything I own. Least you could have done was kept your boxers on or something."

"You know me better than that, Ashy. Underwear's not my thing. Better to keep my options open."

Ash gave me his signature eye roll.

"So what's the plan for the day?" Ash changed the subject. "My parents left some food, but I was thinking of going down to Penny's Market. Maybe grill up some steaks for dinner and watch the ball game?"

"Hell yes. I'm gonna head to the diner for a bit. See if Mom needs anything. But I'll be back in time for steak."

"You want some coffee or food first?" Ash gestured to the half-full pot on the counter.

"Nah, I'll just grab something in town."

I patted down my body, checking to make sure I had my wallet and my sunglasses before walking toward the front door.

"Aren't you forgetting something?" Ash called to me when I was shoving my feet into my weather-inappropriate boots.

I turned to him and sighed in resignation.

"I mean, I didn't think we were gonna be *that* kind of 'roommates,' but if you insist…." I stuck out my lips and made exaggerated kissy noises.

Ash ignored me and dangled a single key off a silver ring.

"Might want to make sure you can get back in. Assuming nobody changes the locks while you're gone, that is."

"Thanks, Papa Ash."

He muttered something at the nickname he hated.

I grabbed for the key chain a split second before moving to plant a sloppy goodbye kiss on his cheek. Which he dodged, the speedy bastard. I guess all the ballet I'd learned from our dancers on tour hadn't made me as nimble as I'd hoped.

Fifteen minutes later I was walking down Main Street, completely in vacation mode. I was enjoying the swirly ice cream cone in my hand, the sun on my face, and the birds nattering in the way they only seemed to do outside of the city. Our cranky band manager, Cory, wasn't around to grump at me over one thing or another.

If there were only a few enthusiastic groupies around this place would be just about perfect. Because that was the thing seriously lacking about Amberwood—hot fucking chicks.

Not gonna lie, even though I loved it, this town had a population with a median age of about eighty-two. Maybe I was exaggerating slightly, but it certainly wasn't far off. Seventy-five years old, minimum. Like, half the population still called my mom "young lady" when she took their orders.

As I got closer to the diner, I took a healthy lick of my ice cream. The motion felt overly sexual for a tasty snack. Was I really that pathetic that I couldn't go more than a few days without sex? I mean, I had… indulged a little while the Thorns had been on tour. It had been so easy to meet incredibly sexy women who literally threw themselves at me in every city we visited. It wasn't like Carter and Beau, our bandmates who both had boyfriends, were at all interested in the European beauties. And even Ash hadn't been coming out with me often lately. So it fell on my shoulders to sacrifice myself to keep up the group's reputation.

Not that I minded.

I shook my head to clear the lusty fog. Perhaps it wouldn't be the *worst* idea to take a break from sex for a while. At least while I was in Amberwood.

A sex sabbatical.

A sexbatical, if you will. Is a sexbatical even a thing?

Focus, Dean.

Why did the nagging voice in my head always sound suspiciously like Ash? I'm sure he would approve of this endeavor; he was always yammering on about how I should be at least a little more selective about the women I took to bed.

I was startled out of my reverie by the cold, sticky ice cream melting down my hand. Looking at the creamy white liquid running over my fingers, I let out a disappointed sigh.

Yup. A sexbatical was exactly what I needed. I licked my fingers, dramatically imagining some metaphorical end to an era.

When I opened the door to the diner where my mom had worked for my whole life, I was hit hard by the nostalgia train. Every cracked-vinyl booth and wobbly chair held dozens of memories of my childhood spent within these greasy turquoise walls. More than almost anywhere else in town, this building was home. The counter I jumped on—and promptly fell off of—when I was finally able to tell Mom that the Thorns had gotten a record deal. The table by the windows where I used to sit for hours on Friday nights as a preteen, absorbing the articles in the *Rolling Stone* magazines I borrowed religiously from the library. The empty wall where the pay phones used to hang, where Mom would fight with my dad during her breaks before he stopped coming around for good. I was fairly certain that nobody on earth loved this place as much as I did.

"I don't see a suitcase, so I'm assuming that means you're not runnin' around town homeless," a voice called from the window connecting the dining room with the kitchen.

"Like you would care if it did!" I sassed.

"Maybe if you'd given me more than five seconds notice, we'd have had a bed for you," Mom said, coming out of the kitchen wiping her hands on a stained white rag.

"It's called a *surprise*! Most people are actually happy to see their long-lost son prodigaling home. Maybe even cry or some shit."

She hugged me tightly against her sturdier-than-it-looked frame. I gave in after a moment, once I'd made it clear that I was *insulted*.

"Good to have you home, Beans," she said, using her childhood nickname for me. "I take it you found somewhere to stay?"

"Yeah, gonna be at Ash's for a while. He's got that massive house all to himself out by the lake."

Theoretically I could have gotten a room in the sketchy hotel off the highway, or even returned to my apartment in New York, but I needed some time back in my hometown while the band was on break. Regroup. Recharge. All that good crap.

"Good. See? It all worked out. You both joining us for brunch this week?"

Ever since I could remember, my mom would make a massive Sunday brunch for the whole family and any assorted friends who happened to stop by. It was an unbreakable tradition, despite whatever escapades of my rambunctious youth had transpired the night before. When money was tight, sometimes brunch was repurposed leftovers from the diner that would have otherwise gone in the garbage. Other times we would sacrifice scratched limbs to pick wild blackberries, or cut the bruises off apples that had fallen on our side of the fence from the neighbor's tree. Whatever we ended up eating, it was always an event. It was the fanciest us Phillipses got, and as I grew older, I realized how much it meant to my mom to pretend for a couple of hours each week.

"I need to ask him, but I'm sure he wouldn't miss it. Want us to bring anything?"

The indignant stare on Mom's face was a far superior answer to what any words could provide. I chuckled at her reaction. Some things never changed.

"Fine, fine!" I put my hands up in surrender. "You can handle it."

"Damn right I can. Now all the business is out of the way, tell me about the tour."

Ash

I HEARD the dead bolt unlock when I was in the middle of seasoning the steaks for dinner. The barbecue was heating after months of disuse, and this new indie band I was currently obsessed with was playing through the speaker system.

"Honey, I'm home!" Dean's voice called through the foyer.

"In here, snookums," I called back sarcastically. "How's the diner?"

Dean appeared in the kitchen and stripped his wallet and phone from his pockets to drop them on the island countertop.

"Good. Mom appears to be fine after the total disownment of her only son. Though we are invited to brunch."

Cherie Phillips's brunches were epic. When Dean and I were in town in December, I was pretty sure I was still full on Tuesday after Sunday brunch. The food kept coming and coming, and even when you were stuffed, it smelled too good to resist eating whatever was brought out next.

"No complaints here. Grab the door?"

I gestured to the screen door, my hands full of the platter of steaks and sauces. Dean ran to slide the door open and lift the lid of the barbecue. Setting the platter down on the side table, I then used a pair of tongs to transfer the meat and tinfoil-wrapped veggies onto the grill. After enjoying the calming sizzle for a second, I closed the top before it lost too much heat.

"I was thinking we'd eat out here? Nice night for it."

Dean glanced at the patio table and chairs I had cleaned and set for dinner. It wasn't anything extravagant, unlike Cherie's brunch spreads, but it was kind of nice to cook for myself after so long eating takeout and whatever the tour venues fed us.

"Damn, Ashy. Remind me again why you don't got a girlfriend? Fancy table, cooked meal? Solid date if you ask me."

The casual word caused me to freeze. Girlfriend. Eventually Dean and I would have to have a conversation, but tonight was not the night. I needed more time.

Recovering quickly, I forced myself to chuckle as Dean took a swallow of the beer he'd found in the cooler I'd stocked earlier.

"On that note, I decided something today," Dean added conversationally.

I was glad for the change of subject before my overanxious mind could spin down the sexuality rabbit hole.

"Oh yeah?" I asked.

"Yup." He nodded. "I've decided I'm gonna take me a sexbatical. Shouldn't be too difficult given the circumstances."

He motioned in the general direction of the center of town, as if I was supposed to understand what he was getting at. I stared at him. I found that sometimes just looking at him blankly for long enough resulted in further explanations as to the magic of the Phillips brain.

"Like a break from sex, you know?" He continued as predicted. "Feel like it's the right thing to do. Was probably going overboard with all the European delicacies."

"I'm sure the ladies of Amberwood will thank you for that."

"Doesn't mean you have to, though. Maybe your Mrs. Wright is already waiting right here. We should see if we can track her down for you while we're home."

"Yup, I'll get right on that," I said, not bothering to react to the age-old pun using my last name. Or the assumed gender of my future spouse.

I flipped the steaks, enjoying the mouthwatering smells when I opened the grill. After grabbing my own beer from the cooler, I took a seat at the table. Dean tapped the neck of his bottle against mine, and we both sat back in comfortable silence, drinking and waiting for the meat to finish cooking. It was an enjoyable night outside, a little hot but cooling off quickly as the sun dipped below the trees. I picked at the damp label of my beer.

"What about Missy Elders?" Dean said, unable to maintain the pleasurable quiet for long. "Mom told me today that she's freshly divorced and looking for love."

I arched my eyebrow. "Doesn't she have like five kids by now?"

"I think it's only three. But I see your point. Lucy Champkin's single."

"You mean my second cousin? Even I'm not that hard up."

"Oh fuck. Yeah, I forgot about that. Guess Amberwood really is that small." Dean chuckled and shook his head.

I took the opportunity to change gears. "I think I'll be fine on my own. But good for you for taking some time out. Seriously," I said as I stood to pull dinner off the grill.

After serving us each a steak, I unwrapped the foil-covered veggies—burning my fingers only a little—and shook half of them onto each plate.

"Looks great, Ashy," Dean told me as he dove in.

I looked down at my own plate, moderately impressed with myself for putting together an edible meal right out of the gate. My cooking ability was usually passable but didn't get much of a workout when we were on tour. It was nice to make food at my own pace when I was at home.

"Oh my God." I groaned deeply as the flavor of the first bite of steak erupted on my tongue. "So fucking good."

Dean paused and gave me a confused stare before blinking and shaking his head subtly.

"Um, yeah. Really good," he stammered uncharacteristically and quickly focused back on his steak. "So you, um, you talk to the guys yet?"

I squinted, not sure what had just happened or why he'd changed the subject so awkwardly. Dean was a weird dude; even if we knew each other the rest of our lives, I didn't think I'd ever figure him out completely. I let it go and didn't call him on it.

"Nah, figured I'd give them a couple days to… settle."

Dean snorted. "Probably smart. Wait for Carter and Chase to come up for air."

I nodded in agreement. Our lead singer, Carter West, had been in a long-distance relationship for the duration of the tour. His boyfriend, Chase, was a few weeks away from graduating from the music composition program at Juilliard in New York. The distance had been incredibly tough on them, but they were childhood sweethearts, and Chase was going to join the Thorns team as our primary songwriter, so at least the separation wouldn't be ongoing.

Dean and I ate and chatted. He seemed a little off all of a sudden, but I couldn't figure out why. It wasn't strange enough to be a huge deal, though for someone who spent as much time with him as I did, it was noticeable. He would stare at me funny, and then when I caught him, his eyes would dart away again. I became a little self-conscious and kept licking my lips to make sure I didn't have sauce on them.

Eventually every morsel on our plates was gone, and Dean stood to start clearing the table. He scooted ahead of me when he realized I was following him, keeping his back turned even when he started speaking.

"We got a few minutes before the game starts. Think I'm gonna grab a quick shower first if that's okay?"

"Yeah, sure," I said slowly. "Might wanna use my en suite. I don't think I put towels in the other bathroom yet. I'll do that tomorrow. Feel free to use my shampoo and stuff if you don't have any. I'll meet you down here when you're done?"

"Cool, cool. Won't be long."

Dean hurried away upstairs without glancing back. Something was definitely strange, but I had no idea what. I shrugged it off and finished cleaning and tidying up the kitchen.

Dean

WINCING in discomfort, I took the stairs two at a time to get to the privacy of the bathroom as fast as possible. I leaned back against the door and exhaled deeply as soon as I had flipped the lock.

What the fuck had just happened?

I stared down at my extremely hard dick, trapped in the confines of my currently-too-tight jeans. Fortunately it didn't seem like Ash had noticed my dilemma. We had been friends long enough that beyond a little ribbing, he wouldn't have cared if he did. Though after that time a few months ago in LA…. Never mind. We'd promised not to talk about that again.

Thinking back, I had no idea what had caused my predicament randomly during dinner. I guess Ash and I had been talking a little about girls, but nothing overtly sexual had come up. Maybe this was, like, a withdrawal symptom? I'd heard of people shaking and sweating after binging on cocaine, so were random boners a consequence of sexbaticals?

As I pulled off my socks, I thought back to the last time I'd hooked up. Probably been more than a week now. Was that long enough for withdrawal to set in? I'd definitely gone longer than that over the holidays last year. And back in March when I'd had that wicked stomach flu. But all the signs were surely leading in that direction. Withdrawal. That's absolutely what this must be.

I quickly stripped off the rest of my clothes and adjusted the temperature gauge, setting it to as cold as I could stand. The frigid water hit my skin when I stepped into the shower and made me recoil. My stubborn cock deflated a little, and I inched the heat up by another degree or two. The decent water pressure cascading down on me did a lot to relax my tense muscles. My jaw cracked open in a wide yawn. Jet lag was starting to set in even though it was still early. The time change and general exhaustion from the tour were messing with my internal clock.

Aware that I didn't have much time before the game began, I shook myself and reached for Ash's bodywash. As I dumped a handful of the gel into my palm, I was hit by the deep, rich sandalwood scent I often attributed to Ash. I rubbed the soap over my chest and arms, the smell intensifying as lather formed. The fragrance clouded my head and overwhelmed my senses. It was heady. Intoxicating.

My dick perked back up, and I moaned a little, unable to hold back. As I washed my way south, the motion of cleaning my balls had my cock practically throbbing.

Did abstaining from sex include jerking off? There was no way I would be able to stop that cold turkey if I wasn't getting any action anywhere else. I thought back to dinner and how uncomfortable it was to be painfully hard under the table, so close to my best friend. Ash's sectional couch was large, but casually popping wood sitting next to him while watching the game didn't seem like a great idea. If my dick wasn't going to cooperate tonight, I would have to take matters into my own hands.

Literally.

I groaned out loud at the dad joke as I fisted my cock.

Adding some more bodywash made the slippery glide feel unbelievably good. My teeth sunk into my bottom lip as I tried to keep my noises to a minimum, not wanting my roommate to become clued in to what was going on in his bathroom. I slapped my other palm against the smooth tiled wall and ducked my head under the spray as I worked myself faster and faster.

It took an embarrassingly short amount of time before the muscles in my legs began to tense as my orgasm closed in over me. An unprovoked image flashed across my squeezed-shut eyes as the first jet of liquid heat struck my palm. Ash's face during dinner with his tongue running along his bottom lip imprinted in my mind like the aftereffect of a camera flash. My body shook and stammered of its own accord, undeterred by the utter commotion in my brain. If anything the tremendous intensity of the orgasm only added to the chaos. It was horrifying... and somehow also satisfying unlike anything I had experienced before.

Eventually my body relaxed. I leaned against the cold wall, panting. Opening my hand, I absently watched the last of my pearly release swirl down the drain.

What the hell just happened?

Once I had recovered, I finished washing my body and my hair quickly, wanting to get away from the scene of the crime and the scent of the sandalwood as soon as possible.

It was hard to deny the fact that I had come with my best friend's—my *male* best friend's—image on my mind. That had to mean something, didn't it? I was totally all for the love-is-love rainbow that seemed to be encompassing my band these days, but I knew myself well enough to recognize that soft skin and a nice pair of tits were what did it for me. I'd never gotten off thinking about a guy before, let alone a friend.

Shit was confusing, and I wasn't sure I could face him immediately after what had happened. I debated making an excuse to hide in my room all night, but I knew Papa Ash would come looking for me, wondering what was wrong. It was a weird blip, that was all. The bizarre result of my incredibly noble sexual hiatus. It didn't mean anything.

I pushed my transgression to the back of my mind and went downstairs to spend the evening with the guy I'd just accidently gotten off to.

Ash

DEAN was still acting odd. Something was off through dinner, and ever since he'd come downstairs after his shower, he seemed to jump a mile every time I looked at him. He was sitting on the far end of the sectional, practically hanging on to the arm for dear life.

"You okay?" I asked. "You're weirder than usual."

"Me? Yeah, totally fine. Maybe you're weirder than usual."

I stared at him out of the side of my eyes and scrunched my face questioningly.

"What? I said I'm fine. Drop it already!" He threw his hands up in the air.

"Woah, chill. I was only asking. Wasn't trying to get your diary key or anything." I showed him my palms, not having any idea where the sudden hostility was coming from.

"Let's just watch the game," he responded with a long sigh.

We sat in silence for a few minutes. Nothing was happening on the TV, so we both pretended to be completely engrossed in the ad for frozen french fries.

"So you think Jefferies is gonna choke again tonight?" I nodded to the screen as it zoomed in on our team beginning their at-bat.

"Not a chance. Last game was a fluke."

"What about the game before that?" I smirked as Dean threw a kernel of popcorn at me. He was far more into baseball than I was. Even though we both supported the same team, I liked to give him a hard time when they were on a losing streak.

Which was most of the time.

"Don't be a dick. Remember that night in Athens when you lost your balance and fell forward into your cymbals?"

I scoffed. "There may have been too much ouzo involved in my preshow warm-up that night," I admitted. "But what's that got to do with Jefferies?"

"Even the badassiest badasses have their off nights, Ashy."

He winked at me, and as if it were scripted, Jefferies connected with the ball, and it soared into the stands beyond the outfield. Dean raised his beer and saluted the TV as I chuckled in disbelief.

By the fourth inning, Dean and I were back on an even footing. We joked and cheered and bullshitted the immature nonsense that tended to come out when Dean and I were together. When I looked up during the seventh-inning stretch, Dean was passed out cold on his side of the couch. After months of living like a rock star, his body was undeniably exhausted. To be honest my eyelids were getting heavy as well.

I shook my head at him and smiled. Dean looked so young and innocent while he was asleep. The subtle lines on his face smoothed, and his smart-talking lips looked almost like a perfect bow at rest. His trademark curls spilled over his forehead, the muscles around his eye twitching from the tickle.

Dean played by his own rules. I'd always liked that about him. Even tonight when something had clearly been bothering him, he never seemed to dwell on the negative for very long. And when he and I were going through that awkward patch after that night in LA, he got over it much faster than I did. I wished I could be so carefree, less like the "Papa Ash" he thought of me as.

Although I secretly liked that he was able to rely on me. It was nice to be needed by someone. By him.

Not wanting to wake him, I gently brushed the curls out of Dean's face. I longed to touch him more, but months ago I had resigned myself to the fact that would never happen again. It was now only a matter of waiting until the desperate longing broke and my heart finally moved on.

Grabbing a soft, chunky knit blanket from the armchair, I covered my sleeping friend so he wouldn't get chilled from the AC. I turned down the lights and the volume of the TV and watched the rest of the game to the music of his soft snores.

THE light was bright behind my eyelids and heat was radiating all down my left side. My foggy brain tried to piece together what was going on. The angle of the light confirmed I wasn't in my bedroom, but I'd lived in so many hotels over the past year, that didn't narrow things down much. My back was stiff like it hadn't had much support overnight.

The heat source threw an arm around my waist and burrowed closer into the nape of my neck. Despite the confusing circumstances, the warm breath was amazing on my skin. I didn't know what was happening; I just knew I didn't want to wake up.

"Mmm," a deep rumble groaned. The arm tightened around me as hips rolled against mine and a hard ridge ground against my ass.

I jerked as if I'd been electrocuted, and my eyes snapped wide open in the same breath. The living room of my house came into focus as my retinas rebelled against the morning sunlight. I shot up to a sitting position, as my unintended bed partner—couch partner?—was startled awake by my movement.

Dean stared at me sleepily for a second before awareness hit and his languid expression was replaced by one of panic.

"Um, good morning?" I forced a smile and attempted to act casual.

"Did I just… uh?"

"Grind your dick against me like you were auditioning for *Magic Mike*? Yup, pretty sure you did."

Dean made a face at my assessment.

"Sorry 'bout that. Must have been dreaming." His eyes flashed open wide—an unreadable expression passing through—and then he added quickly, "You know, about a girl or something."

I nodded, not sure what else to say. Dean sat up and stretched his arms over his head. The move pulled his T-shirt up, exposing a strip of tanned skin along his belly. I stared at the trail of coarse dark hair that disappeared beneath the blanket still wrapped around his hips. The desperate urge to run the back of my knuckle over the exposed skin made me feel like shit.

"Ash?" Dean's voice snapped my eyes up to meet his.

"Sorry, what?"

"Nothing, I just said we must have fallen asleep during the game last night. You know, jet lag's a bitch?" Dean gestured to the TV, which was still broadcasting the sports channel.

"Yeah." I agreed, trying to shake the jittery feeling. "Such a bitch."

I had been doing so well. Ignoring this for so long. But everything was coming roaring back all at once. Why the fuck had I agreed to let him stay with me?

"I might try to grab another hour or two of sleep." Dean yawned loudly.

He stood, the blanket pooling around his feet. The sweats he had on last night were loose and comfortable looking. Subconsciously my eyes shifted to his hips. I tried not to notice the semi he was still sporting before looking away quickly.

"Coffee. Gonna make some coffee," I said, more to myself than to him, as Dean shuffled toward the stairs. I stumbled to the kitchen, mentally scolding myself for what had transpired.

If this was the situation we were in—living together for the foreseeable future—I would need to be more careful.

Dean

I SNUCK back into the guest room at Ash's house, feigning still being sleepy. In reality, I don't think I had ever been more awake. My eyes were wide, and my pulse was thumping a mile a minute. Once was a blip, twice had to mean something. Hands shaking, I fumbled my phone when I went to grab it from the dresser. The battery was almost dead but thankfully still had a little juice left. Pulling up the contact of the first person I could think of, I sent a call before I could second-guess it.

"Come on. Come on, come on, come on," I muttered as I waited impatiently for him to pick up.

Mercifully, the call connected.

"Miss me already?" Jamie's voice was teasing from the other end of the line.

Jamie Griffin was one of the dancers the Thorns had included a few months ago as a late addition to our European tour. He had choreographed a dance to our song "Galaxies" for a showcase at Juilliard, where he was a teacher. He was so fucking talented that the video went viral almost immediately, and our management went apeshit over it. Management brought them onboard for our performance at the *Grammys*, and when that still wasn't enough for the fans, Jamie and another dancer joined us for the second half of our European dates. Not only did he score the heart of our keyboardist, Beau, but he somehow talked me into learning some sick ballet moves from him.

And we became good friends along the way. Who knew ballerinos were such cool guys?

"Jam-Jam, I've got a problem," I whispered into the phone.

Realistically I knew Ash probably couldn't hear me from downstairs; nonetheless, this was a top secret call, and I wasn't taking any chances.

"Everything okay? Say 'Pizza with extra olives' if you're being held against your will," Jamie whispered back. He was mocking me, but little did he know I was about to blow his ginger mind.

"I-think-I'm-in-love-with-Ash," I spat out as one word.

The other end of the phone was silent. Like, terrifyingly silent. Jamie didn't respond for *literally* five minutes.

Okay, it was probably only a few seconds, but it felt like forever.

I checked my phone to make sure the call hadn't somehow hung up.

"Jamie?" I said frantically, needing him to say *something*. "I think I'm in l—"

"Yeah, no, I'm here. I heard you," he cut me off. "Are you serious, or is this like the time you pulled a muscle doing a pli and thought you had appendicitis?"

"WebMD said I should have got it checked out," I said, defending myself and getting sidetracked. I shook my head to clear it. "I've never been in love before. What's it supposed to feel like?"

My voice was small in my ears. Weak and emotional. Afraid.

"Dean, calm down and back up for a sec. You're all about the boobs and legs. What happened?"

"I dunno. We were eating dinner last night, and he just made this sound…."

"Okay, so he was eating and enjoyed the food. So what? That doesn't make you in love with him."

"What about if it made me hard? Like needing-to-have-a-cold-shower hard? And then what if…?" I trailed off, scared to admit the rest.

"What if?" Jamie prompted.

I talked quickly to get everything on the table before I chickened out.

"What if when I got in the shower, the bodywash smelled like him and I couldn't help myself? It happened so fast, and it was so confusing, but it was so damn good. Then we were watching the game last night after, and I think I fell asleep on him. And I'm pretty sure I was grinding against him by accident when we woke up this morning."

"Wow," Jamie said, taking a second before continuing. "Well, I mean, that doesn't sound completely like nothing, but your body reacting sexually isn't exactly the same thing as being in love with Ash either."

"At first I didn't even realize it was because of Ash—or maybe I just didn't want to connect the dots. I'm taking a break from sex right now. To clear my head. I figured this was some sort of weird deprivation thing. But I don't think that's it anymore."

"Have you ever felt something for Ash before this? Or any guy for that matter?"

"No," I answered quickly.

I thought about it for a second and realized that wasn't entirely honest.

"Sort of?" I corrected, hesitating. "There was this one time a few months ago. But there was a girl involved too, so I dunno if that counts."

"Okay, we're gonna talk about *that* later. But I meant more, like, emotionally."

"I dunno. I'm not really a relationshipy, feelingsy guy, Jam-Jam."

"No shit," Jamie said with a laugh.

Another long silence followed. I wasn't good with serious, but this conversation was far from a joke.

"Maybe…," Jamie started and then paused again.

"Maybe what?" I prompted after a few seconds. It was all too much. I was overwhelmed, and I could barely focus.

"Maybe," Jamie continued, more softly than before, "you've been so close to Ash for so long that you've never felt the need to have a relationship."

I sighed and flopped down on the plush mattress, frustrated with myself.

Jamie laughed at my reaction to his psychological assessment, likely assuming I was blowing off the hypothesis. "Fine, fine, maybe that's a stretch."

Was it?

"Let's take this in another direction," he continued. "Maybe you're not in love with him, but you're attracted to him. Are the thoughts you've been having unwanted?"

"No," I groaned in irritation. "I mean it's weird as fuck. But it doesn't feel bad. Or wrong. It's just *Ash.* You know? I'm sure he doesn't feel the same, so it would be super awkward to say anything."

"But what if he does? You two spend a *lot* of time together. You're closer than most couples I know. You've always identified as straight because nobody's made you question that before, so what if it's the same for him?"

"You mean, like, straight except for one person?"

"Exactly. Or a few guys, if that's the case. Maybe even pansexual. It's up to you to define yourself. It just comes down to are you attracted to him?"

Ash

"THAT kick drum you used was insane! The bass you got in 'Galaxies' blew me away!" Brent Tolman, the superstar drummer who had somehow started a conversation with me, said enthusiastically.

It was the night of the *Grammy Awards*, and the Inevitable Thorns had been defeated in the category we were nominated for—ironically for our track titled "Lost." It was hard to mope for long because we'd been invited to play a three-song set, a feat the band had never had the honor of in the past. The set had included our new song "Galaxies." It was a tune we had not expected to become a hit, but a few weeks ago a New York choreographer had crafted a modern dance to the piece that had gone viral. I was no ballet connoisseur; however, even I could admit what Jamie Griffin had created was beautiful.

Once the show was over, my bandmates and I all headed out to Venice Beach for an invite-only afterparty, which is how I ended up casually shooting the shit with Brent freaking Tolman. The guy was a fucking genius, and I was trying my best not to fangirl all over him.

"Thanks, man. Mahogany. Not super common these days, but such a great sound compared to drums made from maple."

"Ah, knew you had to have a secret trick there," Brent said.

We continued on about the effects of different types of wood and manufacturing techniques. It was basically a drum-geek's dream conversation, yet I had to admit that I wasn't fully engaged. I kept getting distracted by the activity on Brent's other side.

Upstanding citizen Dean Phillips was unabashedly hitting on Brent's date, Maddy. She was stunningly beautiful, with long dark hair and perfectly painted red lips that brought attention to her mouth. Her royal-blue gown showed off her petite body to perfection.

And she seemed… into Dean? I tried to focus on Brent, but the flirting and touching between Dean and Maddy was becoming less subtle. Brent had to be aware of what was happening, right? Dean was a grown fucking man. He could do what he wanted, and even though some of our bandmates might disagree, I wasn't his keeper. But this was bloody disrespectful to her date. On both of their parts.

Something was off between Dean and me lately. He invited me to come out with him in almost every city we were in, like he had always done. But more and more I found myself making excuses as to why I wasn't interested in going to clubs or meeting women. Seeing Dean with some of the girls he chased made my stomach tie up in knots. Going out with him went from fun and wingmanish to something I would dread.

I chalked it up to being jealous that he was naturally outgoing and had an easier time picking up girls.

Deep in my gut I knew it was something more than that. Something I wasn't ready to acknowledge.

"Hey, guys, I think we're gonna take off," Carter, our lead singer, said. I hadn't even seen him approach us. His arm was wrapped tightly around his boyfriend, Chase. The two were happy and giggly together; it didn't surprise me at all that they wanted to escape as soon as was socially acceptable.

"Carter West. Fantastic gig tonight, man." Brent shook Carter's hand.

"Hey, Brent. You guys were pretty awesome yourselves," Carter replied. "And congrats on your win. Well deserved."

"Thank you, thank you. Never gets old hearing your name called up there. Tough break for the Thorns. You totally deserved it again this year. Listen, Cart, I don't wanna steal your time away from your guy, but I've got a quick question for you. Can I walk you out?" Brent asked.

"Sure, sounds good. See you boys tomorrow morning?" Carter raised his eyebrows at Dean and me. I knew Carter well enough to realize he was subtly making sure I would watch out for whatever trouble Dean and Maddy got into.

I nodded, once again resigned to my role of Dean's "Papa Ash" for the night.

"We'll be perfect little angels. Right, Ashy?" Dean winked at me.

"Always." I raised three fingers in a Boy Scout salute, playing along even though it made me nauseous.

Carter clapped me on the shoulder and took off with Chase and Brent, leaving Dean, Maddy, and me standing together in an awkward line.

"Don't you want to go with your boyfriend?" I asked Maddy.

"Boyfriend?" She laughed openly. "God no. Brent's my stepbrother. No, I'd much rather hang out here with the two of you."

Ah. Stepbrother. Not a date. That made things slightly better on Dean's part, but still at least a five on the cringey scale.

The three of us chatted for a bit. While I didn't foresee any great romantic attachment between the two of them, there was at least a little more talking than in Dean's usual MO. Maddy and Dean were clearly all over each other, but oddly enough I never felt like the third wheel. They kept me included in their conversation, almost strangely so. She made sure to maintain eye contact when she asked me a question and then leaned in to hear my response over the loud din of the room. After a while, Maddy excused herself to use the ladies' room, and Dean and I made our way to the bar to get refills.

I checked out the rest of the crowd. Being included with the crème de la crème of the music scene was still crazy to me. I scanned the room, wondering where Beau, our keyboardist, had gotten to, finally locating him outside on the patio with Jamie, the choreographer. They looked like they were having an intense conversation. Was something going on between them?

"So what do you think of her? Maddy?" Dean asked casually after we picked up our fresh drinks.

I shrugged my shoulders neutrally. "Seems nice enough. Why?"

"She wants to hook up with us."

I choked a little on the sip I had taken of my gin and tonic. Dean smirked at me.

"Like…?" I waved my pointer finger between Dean and myself.

He nodded slowly.

I took one last failed stab at making sense of this, hoping I had somehow misunderstood. "Separately?" My voice cracked on the last syllable like a fucking teenager.

Dean scoffed and raised his eyebrow at me.

"Really, Ashy? You're that big of a prude? She's *smoking* hot."

I stared at him, trying to formulate words. He had seriously just invited me to have sex with him and some random girl who was on a date—albeit a platonic one—with another guy, as casually as if he was asking for the weather forecast. We were standing in a room with the music industry's elite after the *fucking Grammy Awards*, dressed in our ridiculously expensive loaned tuxes, and he was nonchalantly proposing a two-dude threesome.

And I… fucking hated that I wasn't saying no.

My relationship with Dean had always been so simple. Ever since we had started the Thorns, the two of us had almost always been a package duo. I had no idea why Dean and I had bonded like we had—we were as different as we could be. But somehow when Carter was moaning over Chase and Beau was moaning over Carter, Dean and I had formed our own little rhythm-section brotherhood in the group.

Lately my feelings for Dean had gotten complicated. I would catch his smile out of the corner of my eye, and there were instantly a million butterflies in my stomach. When he touched me casually—as we had always done—goose bumps erupted on my skin. On the nights when we were forced to share a dressing room, my gaze seemed to dart to his body at every opportunity. I lived for our inside jokes, meandering conversations, and random adventures. Our friendship had been built on situations only he and I were privy to. Moments that were once the makings of an innocent friendship had somehow become loaded and intimate.

Why was my mouth so dry all of a sudden? I gulped a sip of my drink.

"Would you and I…?" I didn't know how to ask the really scary question. Didn't know if I wanted his answer to be yes or no.

Would you and I be with each other too?

Mercifully, Dean knew me well enough to fill in the blanks.

"I mean, we'll see each other doing stuff. Focus is obviously on her, though, not that I don't love you the bestest." Dean winked at me.

He was relaxed and fucking around, but that didn't change the effect that his teasing had on me. Still, I couldn't let on that my stomach dropped a little in disappointment. The focus was on the girl. Obviously.

At that moment Maddy sauntered up to us. The leer on her face made it evident she knew what we were discussing. She kissed Dean lightly on the corner of his mouth.

My stare burned into the tiny red mark her crimson lips left behind, unsure about whether I was jealous or turned on.

"So?" she asked.

Dean slipped his arm around Maddy's waist, giving him a second to catch my gaze behind her back. He raised his eyebrows in an unasked question. It was my decision. My pulse pounded. I knew somehow this would change the foundation of our relationship. The trepidation in my belly was overshadowed by the heat licking in my bones and the impossibly hard cock in my Tom Ford silk-trimmed tuxedo pants.

I took a steadying breath.

"I'm in."

Dean

Present Day

ARE you attracted to him?

Jamie's question rang in my ears. Simple words and yet impossibly loaded at the same time.

The tiny Dean in my head was standing in front of two doors. Door one was the simple door. A basic wood-framed pine. I could choose to walk through and pretend none of this had ever happened. Go on with my life. It was the straight man's door, with an endless array of attractive women on the other side.

Door two was far more complicated. It was large and heavy. Dark and enigmatic, with a mysterious sex appeal. It loomed over me. Haze spilled through the cracks.

I rolled my eyes at myself. My fuck, I was dramatic.

"Yes," I answered honestly. "I'm attracted to him."

Definite. Confident. Forthright.

"Well, then, there you go. Congratulations. That's a really big thing," Jamie said.

"So what now?" I asked.

I had conclusively chosen door number two and walked through it, and I breathed deeply a few times before realizing I was now in an infinite hallway of even more doors. An unending corridor of options, filled with self-discovery and new ways to define myself.

Fuck.

Jamie chuckled on the other end of the phone. "That part, I think, is up to you."

"But Jam-Jam!"

I sulked. Jamie only laughed some more and gradually changed the subject. Despite my tendency to joke and sensationalize, I wasn't ready to make my own decisions. I also didn't like to linger on difficult subjects for longer than necessary. It was hard being me.

Conceding defeat at accruing myself some more advice, I let Jamie steer me toward less complicated topics for a while longer.

"You won't, you know, say anything, will you?" I asked as we were wrapping up the conversation.

"Of course not," Jamie promised. "Believe me, I know better than most people how important it can be to keep things under wraps."

I thought back to a few months ago when the press had gotten word of Jamie's relationship with Beau before they were ready. Beau's dad ended up saying some terrible things about them in a tell-all interview on some gossip show, and Beau shut down completely for the better part of a week. I cringed at the memory, the violation.

After hanging up with Jamie, I lay back on the comfy sheets with the comfy pillows and the comfy mattress. That's what Ash had always been for me: comfortable. He never judged me for whatever crazy idea I came up with. He was always there when I got myself into trouble, or made an excuse to get us away when a fan was being overzealous. I could laugh with him more than anyone else on the planet. And when I needed a place to stay—despite plainly having been looking forward to some alone time—he opened his home to me.

But now it was more than that too. For whatever reason, Ash's groans and the appearance of tongue during dinner last night sparked something in me. Despite basically having sex together in LA, I hadn't consciously thought of Ash *sexually*. Sure, he'd always been a good-looking guy, even in high school when he was gawky and hadn't traded his glasses for contacts yet. Nonetheless I'd never once thought of him in a romantic way. Now for the life of me, I couldn't figure out why not.

Sure he was a dude, but I was open-minded. Evidently our bandmate Beau enjoyed a little man-on-man action, even after he'd been with women in the past. Why couldn't I do the same? Thinking about it now, the whole hooking-up-with-a guy-thing seemed kinda new and exciting. Kinda hot. Okay, fine, *really* hot.

I thought about Jamie's word: pansexual. Though I wasn't sure exactly what that meant, I was curious. I grabbed my laptop to do a little research. Where did one learn about specific terms or definitions of sexuality? Wikipedia? Seemed too much like being in school for me.

Did I even care about putting a label on myself?

Fingers hovering above the keyboard in indecision, I eventually typed my favorite porn website into the browser. Experimental learning. Much easier.

Bypassing the boobs, I clicked on the dudes-only section. Overall it wasn't all that different from straight porn. Something for every preference and fetish was readily available. I scrolled through the first page, not turned off by any of the explicit thumbnails, but not really turned on either. How did I know what I would be into?

After five minutes of looking without any luck for something that interested me, I was getting a little frustrated. Pushing myself to jump in, I clicked on the first video that didn't look too extreme. I stripped out of my sweats, ready to enjoy the show. The video began with the same type of cheesy dialogue and horrible acting attributed to all porn. I skipped ahead to where the two guys on screen were making out and feeling each other up. Staring intensely for research purposes, I noted they were both objectively attractive guys, clean-cut and muscly. They seemed to be enjoying each other and had decent chemistry. The camera angles were showing everything that needed to be shown.

Yet it wasn't doing anything for me.

I clicked further into the video. The darker-haired guy was on his knees in front of his partner, going down on him very enthusiastically. I watched for a minute or two as they both moaned and groaned on the screen. My dick remained stubbornly uninterested.

Closing the movie, I chose a different one. Maybe it was just those guys who weren't getting me excited. This clip was shorter, with none of the scene-setting buildup at the beginning. It jumped right in with two guys in the shower going at it. Both of these guys were bigger and hairy; they barely fit into the small shower stall together. It was theoretically hot that two very masculine guys seemed to give no fucks about gender norms; however, beyond a passing allure, I couldn't say they did much for me.

I went through video after video. Frottage, blowjobs, penetration. Twinks and daddies, threesomes, foursomes, real couples that seemed fake, fake couples that seemed real. Leather and lingerie, jocks and cartoons. I stared frustratedly down at my cock, which was half-hard at best.

With a sigh, I shut my laptop and put the computer safely on the small dresser across from the bed. I was about to give up and get dressed again when something caught my attention. A couple of magazines were fanned out on the dresser; the issue of *Rolling Stone* the Thorns had been featured in last year was on top. I flipped through the pages, opening it wide and sitting back down on the bed once I'd found what I was looking for. A centerfold with the four of us hanging out in a backyard pool. I was in the background—midcannonball, of course—with Carter and Beau on giant flamingo floaties, laughing together on the left page. The right page—*the right page*—was Ash stretched out in a lounge chair on the pool deck. Miles of glorious skin were on display; he had one arm casually under his head, wearing only a pair of bright green swim trunks. His eyes were closed, and a peaceful smile lined his lips.

As I stared at the photo, my body reacted far more than it had to the most intimate porn I had just watched. I flipped the left half of the magazine under the right, focusing only on Ash's photo. It was like I was looking at my best friend for the first time. I studied his features.

His strong shoulders built from years of marathon drumming sessions. The endearing dimple on his right cheek when he smiled. The ink that was scattered over his sun-kissed skin. My dick was fully hard now, but I refused to be the creeper who got off to his best friend twice in less than twenty-four hours.

I put the magazine to the side and lounged back against the pillow. As jumbled as everything was in my head, somehow the last hour had helped to clear things up a little.

I wasn't into most guys, but I was definitely into Ash.

Ash

OUR first week off from the tour went quickly. It bled into the second, and then the third. I slept more in those weeks than I had in months. Friends and family came around. Dean and I went to Cherie's brunch every Sunday. Life took on a much slower and simpler pace. I enjoyed it immensely, although I knew it wouldn't be long before I got antsy to get back to music and the band.

Dean and I found a rhythm of living in the same space. We had always gotten along well, and the large footprint of my house gave us each room to do our own thing. I still couldn't figure out what exactly had transpired after we had woken up together on the couch. Dean had bolted immediately after noticing where he was, and a weird vibe had lingered between us for the rest of the afternoon. Since that, we had seemed to regain our equilibrium.

Mostly.

There were times he would look at me in a certain way out of the blue, and it was like somehow *he knew*. I had worked so hard to keep my growing attraction hidden since that night at the *Grammys*, yet these days I was constantly aware of everything I said. Everything I did. Every time I touched him. Dean had always been a tactile guy with everyone. But it was impossible to keep all thoughts of him at bay when he would reach over to massage my neck after dinner or sit close enough for our shoulders to make contact when we were watching TV. Or like the other day when he bought me an out-of-print record from this band I was obsessed with back in high school, which he had stumbled across in a secondhand store. Dean had always been generous, but he had never done something so thoughtful before. Not for anyone else and certainly not for me.

I honestly wasn't sure what to do about the whole thing, so I kept doing what I had done for months: I ignored it. After a lot of soul-searching on tour—and one night in Leeds that made everything completely obvious—I knew I wasn't straight. I would have had no problem coming clean about that fact if it wasn't for the most inconvenient crush in the world. Once I got over Dean, I would tell my family. And the band.

Maybe then I would be able to actually date someone. *Who* I would find to date remained to be seen. The population of Amberwood, let alone the *gay* population of Amberwood, was tiny. Or at least I assumed the gay population must be tiny. If I couldn't date in Amberwood, and I couldn't date anyone seriously when we were touring, what did that leave? My bandmates seemed to be pairing up at an alarming rate, and deep down I longed to have someone to spend my life with in the same way. The same way my parents had.

My parents were in the ideal scenario. Their mutual passion for music connected them in a way most people only dreamed of. They'd played in the symphony together from a young age and were stupidly happy spending most of the waking day in each other's presence. The chances of that happening to me were basically impossible. Unless I magically started dating someone who was a part of our road crew. Or someone from a band who opened for us.

The sun was setting late in the evenings these days. Dean had been at the diner all day and hadn't come home yet, so I had eaten by myself and long since cleaned up. I located the weathered violin case next to the piano in my small music nook and headed out onto the back, west-facing deck to enjoy the sunset. The violin was one of the first instruments I learned to play, given both of my parents played it professionally. All these years later, I was still enamored with the rich, sensuous sound. It wasn't an instrument that fit into the music the Thorns played, and space on the buses and trucks was always limited, so my violin never traveled with me. However, I tended to gravitate toward it when I was at home.

I clicked open the case on my patio table, running my fingers lightly over the stretched strings. I tightened my bow and picked up the instrument. With my chin resting on the smooth spruce frame, I brought violin and bow together, waiting for musical inspiration to strike. Without conscious thought, I began to play.

It was a sweet, melodic song that I couldn't think of the name of even after beginning. My fingers found the notes on their own, and the motion of bow on strings sent beautiful tones soaring into the sunset. It wasn't until I was halfway through the tune I realized I was playing a string version of "Next to Me," one of our band's biggest hits. I had never played the song on my violin before—it just seemed to come pouring out of me.

I lost track of time, playing whatever came out of my fingers: classical pieces, rock songs, stuff from the Thorns's catalog. Each tune blended effortlessly into the next. After a while, I heard the screen door open and close. Dean appeared and sat in the chair beside me. We acknowledged each other's presence with a smile and then went back to staring into the darkening backyard. He listened to me play without making a sound, seemingly enjoying the peace and music as much as I did.

When my unaccustomed fingers could take no more of the rigid strings, I laid my violin back in its velvet case. Dean let out a relaxed sigh.

"I sometimes forget how talented you are, Ashy," he said, finally breaking the silence.

I shrugged off the compliment. "Genes, I guess."

Dean shook his head, looking into my eyes. Into my soul.

"Maybe a little. But it's more than that. You're so dedicated. So loyal to what you do. To us. You could do whatever you wanted."

I scoffed and rolled my eyes, unnerved by how uncharacteristically serious Dean was being. My defenses rose to protect my heart, but everything was raw. The moment was like kindling, ready to ignite with the smallest flame. I was scared to look at him, scared of what would happen if I returned his solemnity. Scared that he would pull the rug out from under my feet and make a dumb joke. Scared that this game of chicken we had been playing would finally prove itself to be no more than a punchline.

Eventually I raised my gaze. His dark eyes were locked on mine. The fire sparked.

"What are we doing?" I whispered, terrified of the answer regardless of what it turned out to be.

"I don't know," he said simply.

And then he kissed me.

Ash

Grammys Night. Los Angeles, California

"WELL, that was new," Dean said as he appeared from the steamy bathroom, ruffling a towel through his hair to dry his curls.

The second tiny towel he had precariously knotted around his hips seemed to be tempting gravity. I averted my eyes, not trusting them to keep my secrets given Dean's current state of undress.

I cleared my throat, which was suddenly thick with emotion.

"Uh, yeah." I nodded awkwardly. "Maddy had to go. She said to tell you she had a good time."

I ignored the other part of my brief exchange with her while Dean had been in the shower. The part where she had given me a knowing look. Her eyes burned into the depths of my soul, and I knew she knew. She knew without me having to say a word and without asking me a single question. I think she assumed she was doing me a favor by taking off, giving me—giving *us*—time to process. In reality, the gaping hole her absence left in the hotel room made things a thousand times more uncomfortable.

Uncomfortable for me at least. I wasn't convinced Dean knew the meaning of the word.

He stripped the towel off his hips and squatted over his suitcase, ass in the air and balls dangling between his legs. It should have been the least attractive visual in the entire world, but fuck if looking at the firm curve of his ass didn't make my cock perk up again.

I shifted to conceal it. Willed myself to calm down. I should probably leave, right? This was the part where I left and we never—*never*—talked about this again.

Why couldn't I force myself to get out of bed?

Dean finally fished a pair of black athletic shorts out of his disaster of a suitcase—how he had managed to mangle it so badly after a single day was anyone's guess.

"Eh, that's cool." Dean turned to face me, giving me the full monty. Suddenly the generic hotel room artwork above his head required all of my attention. "You hungry? I could go for some pie or something."

He stepped into the shorts, and I let out a small sigh of relief. The situation wasn't much better with his sexy, tatted-up torso still on display, but it was something.

"Sure. Yeah. Pie's good," I said. I was stuttering and spewing like one of those computer loading screens that paused at 40 percent forever and then jumped to complete in one go.

The truth was, the fuzzy, abstract concept I had been sitting on for the past few months had come into indisputably sharp focus tonight. It was scary and yet extraordinarily calming at the same time. I finally had the beginnings of an answer.

But the answer was terrifying.

I had somehow developed a crush on my bandmate.

My best friend.

My *straight* best friend, who literally could not be more of a womanizer if he tried.

It was an interesting train of thought. I had always considered myself to be straight as well, yet I was more concerned about Dean's sexuality than my own. Now that I thought about it, the whole thing seemed ridiculous. There was no way I was gay. I had always been into women. So what if it usually took some convincing to get my dick into the game when I brought a girl back to my hotel room? That was just nerves. Or because I'd had a drink or two after the show. It happened to every guy. Right?

"Ash!"

"Huh?" I shook my head to focus, wondering how long Dean had been calling my name.

"I said did you want apple, pecan, or strawberry rhubarb?" Dean asked, pointing to the cell phone at his ear.

"Oh, um. The last one," I answered, not caring in the slightest about pie flavors at this particular moment.

Dean went back to the call, relaying the order to the room-service staff.

His mouth moved, but the words didn't register. I watched his lips. The lips that had just kissed their way down Maddy's body in the way I wished they had floated down mine. How I longed to kiss those soft, dirty-talking lips. I watched his Adam's apple bob in his throat. So distinctly masculine. I imagined licking it, distracting him while he was on his call. Feeling the scratch of his stubble along my cheek at the same time. I watched his hands. His rough musician's hands he gestured with as he spoke. The hands that accidently brushed up my leg during an intimate moment when they should have been focusing on her. The hands that unexpectedly didn't move away once he realized it was my thigh he was touching.

Watching Dean with Maddy tonight had been a lesson in intimacy and self-control to the highest degree. Balancing on the knife's edge between letting myself relax and doing what I wanted to be doing— touching him—versus what I should be doing with her. Never fully letting my guard down. That moment when she was on her knees in front of him and Dean's eyes locked with mine. It took everything I had not to sink to the ground and insist I be the one to bring him pleasure.

It was the first time in a long time I had been able to perform at all. I hated myself for that.

"Ash!" Dean said loudly again, waving a hand in front of me.

I blinked, his face coming into focus.

"What's with you tonight? It's like you keep getting lost in your own head. Was it…?" Dean gestured at the mussed-up bed with an unasked question.

"No," I said quickly, brushing off the lingering awkwardness and trying harder to concentrate. "Nah, I'm good. Just tired. Long day."

Ironically, it was the same excuse I'd used countless times before with women I'd brought home.

Dean quirked his eyebrow like he was trying to figure out whether to believe me.

"I'm good," I insisted.

"Okay," he said skeptically. "I know I kinda talked you into it, but if it was weird or anything—"

"It wasn't weird," I cut him off. "You didn't force me to do anything. I wanted to."

"You sure? 'Cause that was really fucking hot."

"Yeah." I nodded, trying to appear convincing. "Really hot. But like, we're gonna keep that between us, right?"

I needed to bury this. Never think about tonight again. Dean's lack of filter would make that next to impossible if he wanted to talk about it, or worse, make jokes.

"Like, the guys might be weirded out knowing we did that with Brent's sister. Bro code and all." I argued my point, making up the reasoning on the spot.

Dean grimaced; his expression made me chuckle.

"Yeah, best be keeping that one from the guys. Cart would probably try to analyze the shit out of us doing that together," he said.

I shuddered at the thought of how *that* conversation would go. Sweat started to prickle my skin. I suddenly became fascinated with the hangnail on my thumb, unable to meet his gaze again. "It, um, it was just a weird onetime thing anyway. Was only 'cause she wanted to. Didn't mean anything. Right?"

My chest was tight with anxiety, knowing there was only one correct answer here. Somehow still hoping for a different one.

"Right, right." Dean's response came painfully hurried. Fast and direct, leaving no room for interpretation. I was probably imagining the hint of disappointment in his quick words.

A knock at the door made us both jump. Dean went to pick up our room service, leaving me painfully aware of how close we had been standing even after what had transpired. I took a breath, willing my fight-or-flight response to chill the fuck out.

We ate postsex pie and watched the tail end of a ball game on the massive TV. Dean smack-talked both teams enthusiastically. I threw in the occasional comment so he wouldn't think anything was up. A short time later, we exchanged a semiawkward goodbye, and I went back to my own room.

Despite the late hour, my brain refused to turn off and let me sleep. My thoughts were a mess of muscled forearms and masculine groans. Tonight had been supposed to help me get over whatever it was that I had been curious about, but it ended up having the opposite effect. Dean and I had far too many months left on tour in each other's direct proximity for things to be weird between us. I would make an effort to push all these uncomfortable feelings aside.

How difficult could that be?

Dean

IN the three weeks since my call with Jamie and my resulting private experiments, I had made an effort to notice Ash. I watched as he spent evenings hunched over a textbook in the dining room, hell-bent on graduating college online despite the crazy schedule Thorns kept. I watched him interact with the kids at the Amberwood Elementary School when we popped into their music class as special guests. He was so good at answering their questions as they excitedly swarmed us, the unintentional local celebrities. I watched him banter amicably with my mom over Sunday brunch each week. I watched his face light up when I did something nice for him or gave him a gift.

As relaxed as I was about sex, potentially starting something with Ashy was a really big deal. I didn't take much seriously, but Ash meant the world to me, and even I wasn't stupid enough to risk our friendship for an experimental fuck.

I had debated what to do for a few weeks, but arriving home and hearing Ash's beautiful violin music from the driveway was somehow the final push I needed. When I joined him on the deck, I was enveloped in soulful melodies and the intimate parts of Ash's talent he shared with so few people. The music transported me to a simpler time, to when the Thorns were nothing more than a group of four high school friends who loved to play. Sharing big dreams that seemed too impossible to come true.

Ash eventually put his instrument back into its case and shook out his fingers.

"I sometimes forget how talented you are, Ashy," I said.

He shrugged. "Genes, I guess."

I shook my head and looked at him. Really looked at him.

"Maybe a little. But it's more than that. You're so dedicated. So loyal to what you do. To us. You could do whatever you wanted."

He rolled his eyes, maybe a little embarrassed by my much-deserved compliments. When he shifted his gaze back to me, everything got real. He looked at me like what I had been feeling recently might not have been one-sided after all. Like somehow this strange pull between us was affecting him too.

"What are we doing?" he whispered, eyes big and scared.

"I don't know," I replied.

I wasn't sure who kissed who first. All I knew was that the tension between us finally broke. Like the first sheet of rain in an epic thunderstorm. One second the air was muggy and thick, almost impossible to breathe. Then the crash came, and out of nowhere we were in the heart of the downpour. It was unfamiliar and a little disorienting—a shock to the system—but all I wanted to do was dance. I'd had an embarrassingly large number of kisses in my life so far. Never before had one been like a bolt of lightning.

The kiss turned from tentative to something deeper. He nibbled my bottom lip. I ran my tongue over the seam of his, begging for entrance. Ash's end-of-day stubble abraded my face, make it undeniable it was a man I was enjoying. It was new and different but in an erotically exciting way. We explored each other with needy moans and needier hands. Once the initial urgency had passed, a new fear hit me. As soon as the kiss ended, we were going to have to *talk* about this. Talking would make it real.

Ash grabbed for the bottom of my T-shirt, running his fingers tentatively over the hem. Oh.

Oh.

Maybe he didn't want to talk at all.

I was usually all for taking things quickly when the opportunity presented itself, but somehow I had assumed things would move slower with Ash. A kiss in itself wasn't usually my end goal, yet this kiss was overwhelming enough on its own.

He pulled back a fraction, not saying a word but looking at me with the question in his eyes.

I knew we would need to talk at some point. Stopping here for discussion was the right thing to do. But the way he looked at me—with so much vulnerability, so much want—made every rational thought disappear from my mind.

As unsure as I was, I nodded to Ash, giving him all the permission he needed. Not wanting to reject his advances if I only got one shot at this.

He stripped the thin cloth over my head. The cool night air was wonderful on my exposed skin, but nowhere near as good as Ash's hands running over me. I let him explore. His fingers were timid to begin with, growing more confident with each passing moment. I remained motionless, terrified that if I moved even a fraction, Ash would shake himself out of this heady moment and stop. That he would remember we weren't supposed to be doing this. That we were straight.

Or at least he probably was.

I had no idea about myself anymore.

All I knew was I wanted this. Him. More than I had ever wanted anyone before.

His hands ran over my back, my shoulders, my neck. He stroked my jaw with his thumb. I nipped his finger when it got close enough, circling my tongue over the pad of his digit and sucking it into my mouth.

Ash whimpered quietly, almost inaudibly. The sexy sound made my breath hitch. Made my cock swell so fast my head got light. Our eyes locked. His smoldered with lust and desire and hunger.

And it was on.

No more hesitating. No more uncertain touches. We both wanted this. Needed it. *Craved* it.

For right now at least.

I stood, grabbing Ash around his middle and pulling him upright with me. My mouth took his in a bruising kiss. I wrapped my arms around him aggressively, smashing our bodies together as close as we could get.

The logistics of kissing someone taller than me took some adjusting, but I wasn't going to let that impede the embrace for even a second. Ash must have had the same thought, as he began to back me through the screen door and into his living room.

We fumbled blindly for the couch. I managed to fight the shirt off him just before my legs collided with the cool leather. I yanked Ash down on top of me, blanketing my body with his. It was messy and unrefined, us clawing at each other in an encounter that would surely leave marks. The scent of sandalwood made my head cloudy, surrounding me with *Ash*. It was like it had been in the shower, only this time the smell was so much more than suds and lather. I'd never been so free before. Ash was a wall of muscle and strength— no need to be gentle or hold back with him.

His body moved frantically against mine, seeking kisses. Seeking friction. The solid ridge behind Ash's zipper was impossibly good grinding against me. I rolled my hips, taking in the new sensation. If there was any doubt at this point, that ridge was irrefutable proof that he wanted this as much as I did. There was something powerful in knowing I was turning him on.

My pulse was fluttery and unstable. Part of me wanted to slow us down from the lightning-fast pace we had set. Maybe take the time to enjoy the scenery a little. But then Ash kissed his way down my neck, accidently finding the spot below my ear that made me fucking crazy.

Nope. There would be no view-seeing for us.

At least not during this round.

I moaned shamelessly at the heat of his lips. At the delicious scrape of his stubble. I reached for the buckle on his jeans, honestly not sure if I had time to get us out of our pants before I hit the point of no return. Ash did little to help the situation. He clung to me so tightly it was nearly impossible to squeeze my hand between us to fiddle with buttons and zippers.

Grunts and groans filled the room as Ash's hips snapped faster, losing their rhythm. I gave up on his belt, needing to see his face more than his cock as I realized we were both seconds away. Fuck. I hadn't come from fully clothed dry humping since… ever. Not even in an awkward high school fumble.

Ash's mouth never left my neck. He alternated between biting and licking and caressing the delicate skin in a way that was somehow directly linked to my cock. Every second I lasted was a feat. As desperate as I was to come, I wanted this to go on forever.

"Look at me, Ashy," I said, forcing the strained words out.

As incredible as his mouth was, his head buried in the crook of my neck wasn't what I needed in this momentous moment. I needed him to see me. To watch as I fell apart and know it was *me* he was making feel so good.

Ash pushed his chest up slightly. His breath was hot on my skin, his winter-gray eyes inches from my own. It was everything I never knew I needed.

His hips stuttered, and his mouth opened in a broken sob. It was the sexiest thing I had ever seen in my life. My release hit me hard a beat behind his. The ground fell away under me and my entire being—not just my body, but my *being*—shook with pleasure. He stared at me as his strong hands gripped my hips, anchoring our lower bodies together. I stared at him as every muscle contracted until my orgasm eventually released its hold.

Our harsh breathing was the only sound in the room. My thoughts slowed, and all that was left was feeling. Feeling my body melt into the cushions, completely relaxed and sated. Feeling Ash's chest draped over me like a comforting weighted blanket. Feeling calm. Happy. Right. Feeling so immensely satisfied.

Feeling Ash's body stiffen, fracturing my blissful bubble.

Ash broke eye contact, suddenly looking everywhere except at me. I could sense him slipping away. From me. From what we had just done. Panicking, I reached to touch him, to rub my hands over his back and help him calm down. He jumped up from the couch like it was on fire, retreating to the adjoining kitchen. Putting space between us. His hands scrubbed over his face. Looking down, he refastened the belt I had barely managed to unbuckle. He couldn't get away from me fast enough.

I sat up a little, still wrung out and slow. It wasn't often that I saw my beautiful best friend so unsettled. He was the steadfast, dependable one. I was the unreliable flight risk of the band.

The burst of adrenaline and alarm because of Ash freaking out woke me up a little. As I shifted, the wet stickiness in my pants became more noticeable. It had been one of the most intense orgasms I could remember, and there was an awful lot of come down there. My sexbatical had been shot to hell, but there was no way I would ever regret what had transpired.

Unless of course Ash did.

Ash

"**UM,** what just…," I began and stopped just as quickly. "That was… uh…."

My voice was shaky as I ran my fingers through my hair. I paced back and forth, the mess inside my pants adding to the general squirminess of the situation.

"Ashy," Dean said gently, appearing before me.

He was relaxed and composed, with a shy smile lifting one side of his lips. Lips that I had spent the last half hour obsessed with. Lips that tasted sweeter than strawberries fresh from the field in the middle of August. Lips that made me harder than I'd ever been in my life. A fresh wave of terror hit me at the thought. I forced myself to look away.

This was *Dean*. Not just a *guy*, but my bandmate. My best friend. The guy I had been trying to avoid thinking about for months. Someone I knew better than anyone else. Our lives were forever connected by the Thorns. Out of all the people in the world to take a romantic gamble on, I was choosing *Dean*? I had seen this man take groupies home with him literally dozens of times in the last eight months. Every city. Every type of woman imaginable. Dean loved sex. Loved experimenting with sex. And that's all I was to him here. Like the threesome in LA. Another experiment.

"Ash," Dean said again. "Look at me."

I wasn't sure whether he realized he was mirroring the words he'd used a few moments before, but I certainly noticed. Those words—and the subsequent penetrating stare—had made me come harder from a little fully clothed frottage than from the previous hottest sex of my life. Dean's expressive brown eyes were directly connected to his soul. They had an intense hold on me. In the heat of the moment and now.

"We shouldn't have done that," I whispered.

I took a breath, willing the moisture in my eyes to disappear before he caught on. The words were the last ones I wanted to say, but the only ones that would protect me.

He lightly touched my forearm. The simple contact was both comforting and electric at the same time. Meeting his gaze, I tried to quell the need to shuffle or run.

"Did that feel good?" he asked simply.

Did it feel good? That was the first thing that came to his mind? What kind of a stupid fucking question was that? *Did it feel good?*

Did he not notice how I was humping him like an overwrought Chihuahua back there? That I couldn't even get my pants off before I came as if a goddamn fire hydrant exploded?

Did it feel good.

Pfft.

Feeling good was *so* not the point here.

The look on my face must have portrayed my sarcastic train of thought, as Dean began chuckling. "Okay, fine. So it felt good! It felt good for me too. Felt fucking amazing if we're being honest." He carried on, picking up speed with every word. Gesturing wildly with his arms as he spoke. Dramatic and overexaggerated as usual.

"But it doesn't have to be a big thing if we don't want it to be." His tone changed suddenly. He broke eye contact. It looked like there was a question there, but it was too fleeting for me to dissect. "It felt good, we got off, end of story."

It was clear he only thought of this as a hookup.

The past half hour represented so much more to me. In my entire life I'd never been so free. Sex had always been the cause of an enormous amount of worry and angst. And this time I had just… jumped. Led with my body. My heart. My overzealous brain relegated to the back seat for once. There had been no anxiety. No performance stress. No embarrassing excuses as to why I couldn't get it up.

That was how sex was *supposed* to be. I'd spent more than a decade of my life wondering why everyone around me seemed obsessed with sex. It had never consumed me. I'd never understood the appeal. Sex was mediocre at best. It happened, it was okay, and then it was over.

But now I finally had an explanation. Every lackluster encounter in my past suddenly made sense. I'd known for a while I was attracted to guys, but I was 100 percent sure now that I was gay. This made sense to me. There was no way I could go back to being with women after this.

Hell, Dean and I had barely even done anything and it was incredible! If we'd progressed any further than that, I probably would have gone into cardiac arrest!

The burden I'd carried for so long began to melt away. I was *so* fucking gay.

My eyes regained their focus, and Dean was still there, staring at me expectantly. Waiting for me to say something.

My chest deflated as I played what he'd said over in my head.

It doesn't have to be a big thing.

Oh.

Reality returned quickly. While one weight was lifted off my shoulders, a larger one was added.

It felt good, we got off, end of story.

I searched Dean's eyes for an answer, trying to piece together what he wanted me to say here. How to protect myself and shrug off the whole thing like he was able to do so easily. How to go back to being regular old Dean and Ash. If we could ever be that again.

"Yeah." I forced a smile. "It doesn't have to be a big thing."

Dean nodded.

"Listen, um, I gotta take care of this situation." He exaggeratedly made a circle in the air over his crotch.

I forced a laugh, my attention drawn back to the mirroring stickiness in my own jeans.

"Yeah, I could probably do with a shower," I said.

Dean quirked his eyebrow at me.

"A separate shower. You in one shower. Me in a separate—*far away*—shower," I clarified.

"What if I promise not to look?" he teased.

"No."

I lightly shoved him in the direction of the guest bathroom he had begun using.

"Come on! I'll keep my eyes north of the border. Like, remember I told you about that chick I hooked up with who had the janky-ass tattoo of the band on her hip? Us all as robot zombies or something? Scared the shit out of me. Same thing." He gestured to the top half of his body. "Eyes up here the whole time."

I grabbed a fresh towel from the linen closet as we walked by and pushed it into Dean's hands.

"As flattering as that comparison is, I'm gonna have to pass. You. Go." I pointed into the bathroom, shooing him inside.

"Or I could look, if that's what you would prefer. Nothing to be ashamed of between friends. It felt like you have a really big—"

I slammed the bathroom door shut behind him before I was forced to hear the last word of his sentence.

Slumping against the closed door, I fought the urge to bang my head against it. I listened, waiting until I heard the water turn on. Once I was sure I was alone, I took a shaky breath and headed to my en suite to deal with the aftermath.

Dean

WE shouldn't have done that.

Ash's words hit me like a punch in the stomach. All the amazing sex-endorphins flooded out of my system, and the nausea crept in.

When I went to Ash in the kitchen, I was prepared to go in with some very un-me real talk. To lay down how I had been feeling recently and see if there was any chance he might reciprocate. But Ash was panicking, and so I defaulted to my status quo: make a joke and keep the sex casual.

The worst part was, I couldn't tell if he meant it or if he was merely protecting himself. Either way made me feel like shit.

It hurt.

It felt like I had taken advantage of him, even though rationally I knew he'd instigated taking things as far as they went. What we did was equal. Consensual. He was just flipping out now that it was done and he'd had time to think.

I brushed his words off, unsure of what else to do. Making Ash happy was my priority. I would deal with my own feelings later. For a second or two, it seemed like he wanted to say something else. I left the door open. A desperate last Hail Mary.

It doesn't have to be a big thing if we don't want it to be.

I want it to be, Ash. I want it to be the *biggest* thing. But he didn't.

Maybe he was afraid or just in his head too much—that happened to Ash a lot. The moment passed, and we agreed to put it behind us. If Ash didn't want to talk about it, I wasn't going to force him to. I already carried enough guilt about the situation.

Things were icy between us that evening—and not in the delicious popsicley way. I wanted to give Ashy some space to think, some time to be by himself without worrying about running into me in his own home. So the next day I called up my sister Harlow and invited her and my niece, Gracie, to the petting zoo with me. Harlow and Gracie had recently moved back to Amberwood and were living with my mom, which was the reason I was staying with Ash in the first place. I wasn't really sure what level of amusement an eight-month-old would get from such an endeavor, but I wanted to enjoy the limited time I had with her while I was in town. Plus what rational adult didn't love the excuse to go to a good petting zoo?

"Gracie wants to ride the llama?" I asked, holding her above the caramel-colored fluffer.

"No, she doesn't!" Harlow said, right on cue. I winked at my sister, enjoying getting to tease her. Harlow cooed at her daughter and took Gracie from me. I pouted—like I would ever let anything bad happen to my niece.

"It's a petting zoo, not a riding zoo," Harlow sing-spoke to Gracie, indirectly scolding me in the process.

"But it could be both if we just believe!" I argued. "Come on! It's a great new business idea. Completely untapped market. Uncle Dean and Gracie's Riding Zoo. We could have llamas and sheeps and alligators. Maybe a penguin or two. Though penguin-riding insurance might be high. Someone could slip and fall on the ice."

"Right. Though I'm sure alligator-riding insurance would be reasonably priced."

Harlow shook her head, reminding me of how Ashy tended to react to me when I had a brilliant idea. The thought of Papa Ash made me smile.

The three of us walked past the llama pen into a grassy area with baby goats. They were seriously adorable, and I immediately crouched down to play with them. Maybe the petting zoo was more for me than for Gracie after all. Who could be worried about minor problems with gray-eyed drummers when there were baby goats in the world?

Harlow bent down next to me with Gracie on her hip. I showed my niece how to pet the bleating beast.

"Has Adrian been coming around?" I asked. The bitterness in my voice about Gracie's deadbeat father was more evident than I'd intended, but seriously, fuck that guy. Adrian was bad news from the time Harlow met him, and he'd had one foot out the door from the moment the second line appeared on the drugstore pee test. Gracie deserved so much better.

Harlow deserved so much better.

"Sometimes." Harlow hesitated. "Not really."

I scoffed.

"I've, um, sort of been seeing someone…," she said tentatively.

My shoulders tensed. Harlow's dating life, even before Adrian, had been questionable at best. She had a type, and that type was no good. Harlow had liked her boys bad from the time she was in high school—a string of guys who wore leather jackets, rode motorcycles, and made *very* questionable choices when it came to hairstyles. I had hoped that now that she had a kid, things would change. But my sister was a Phillips through and through, and we were all an incredibly stubborn lot.

"It's not what you think," she said, noticing my tension. "Do you remember Jimmy Feldman? He was the year below you in school."

My eyes went wide in surprise. The image of the nerdy band geek's face appeared in my mind. Jimmy lived down the block from us growing up. Until the Thorns had become friends, Jimmy and Ash were tight, and he had always trailed Harlow around like a puppy, even though she was younger than him. He dressed in hand-me-downs that were decades out of style and had a serious case of the smells through puberty. Kids were mean, and he had gotten bullied, but Jimmy was confident beyond his years and kept his head held high. I remember hearing he had gone to some fancy college in Boston for math. Or physics. Or some other smart-people subject. I couldn't remember exactly.

"No way! You're dating Smelly Feldman?"

"Yes, and don't call him that. He goes by James now." Harlow unlocked her phone and held up a photo of her and an attractive man who looked nothing like the scrawny nerd I knew.

"Wow, Smelly grew up gooood…."

Harlow rolled her eyes.

"He's been staying with his parents down the road. Helping out. His dad's having some health issues. He started checking in on Gracie, bringing us meals and watching her for a few minutes so I could get some things done around the house. Gracie loves him. It was nice to have him around. He's always been so good to me. So one day I just leaned over and kissed him," Harlow said with a bashful smile.

One of my little goat buddies started butting his head into my leg, probably wondering why the pats had stopped. Harlow's sweet story had distracted me to the point of goat neglect. I reached down to begin stroking his stiff fur again.

"That's great, Low," I said, using the nickname I'd always called my sister. "I'm happy you finally have someone who treats you the way he should."

She nodded as she played with Gracie's teeny-tiny fingers. Gracie hadn't exactly been planned, but I had always had hope that she'd been a blessing in disguise for Harlow.

"You deserve to have that too," Harlow said, looking up at me expectantly. "A relationship. A partner."

Crap. Walked right into that one, didn't I? Happy couples recruited others to join their ranks more frequently than the army.

The only difference was for the first time in my life, I could almost see myself being converted.

"We should move on, make sure Gracie gets to see all the other animals," I said, weakly attempting to change the direction of the conversation. "I bet there are some big fat rabbits over there, Gracie! Did you wanna see the bunnies?"

Making a big display of being excited, I tickled Gracie's belly so she laughed at me. Taking the baby back into my arms, I hopped down the trail to the next exhibit, ignoring Harlow's muttered comment about my sex life mirroring that of a rabbit.

Some jokes were too easy to bother dignifying with a response.

Ash

THE day following "the incident," Dean decided to escape the house for a few hours. He invited me out with him, but I said no. It was obvious that he made plans at the last minute so he could avoid me for a few hours and was only asking out of politeness.

Also, what kind of a grown-ass man thought the Amberwood Petting Zoo was the pinnacle of entertainment?

Unsure what to do with myself, I wandered aimlessly around the big empty house for a while. I turned on the TV, but there was nothing good on. I sat down at my piano, but inspiration never struck. Eventually I settled at the large kitchen table with my nineteenth century world history textbook, opening to chapter seven to get ahead on some reading for next week's online lecture.

History had always interested me nearly as much as music. I loved the concept of technology and transformation throughout the ages. What now seemed mundane and routine had once been a groundbreaking revolution. We took so much for granted today; it was fascinating how people once lived so simply. There was very little chance I would ever need my history degree to pay my bills, very little chance I would use it at all down the road. I could never do more than one or two courses at a time, and it would likely take fifty-seven more years to complete my degree. Despite all this, for some reason every semester—regardless of whatever the band had going on—I enrolled in more classes.

Most people probably thought I was crazy for doing it. I regularly got into strange situations, because even though it was rare for my face to be recognized in a crowd, people did recognize my name. I'd had autograph requests from TAs more than once. My college-issued email address had to be changed and hidden from contact lists after a classmate shared it on Twitter. I'd been asked to turn off my camera in several courses because apparently it was a distraction for some students. Last semester, two days before the start of session, I got an email saying I had been withdrawn from a degree-required class. I frantically called admissions during our soundcheck in Belgium to figure out what had happened. Turns out the teacher saw my name on the attendance list and, assuming it was a joke, deregistered me.

It still mystifies me why someone would pay thousands of dollars in tuition to register in a class as a joke. But whatever.

I was so used to blending in with the background, being the least recognizable of the band. It was weird to me when someone noticed me without any other Thorns or any context other than my name. Dean loved when I told him stories about ridiculous situations at school. He got a kick out of me being confused why I got special treatment.

Being a famous student wasn't all fun and games. Last year I mortifyingly had to request an extension on a paper—the only time in my entire academic career that had happened—because the band had some technical problems during rehearsal for the *American Music Awards*. Our touring schedule had been crazy, and we were supposed to have the afternoon off. I had planned to finish the paper then, as it was my only opportunity, but our sound was a mess, and the producers were all flipping out. We had to continue rehearsing right up until showtime to get it right. My professor had been understanding about the situation but still deducted a full letter grade for my tardiness. It was the lowest mark I got in the class, which bothered me endlessly. I hated to use the rock star card to get special treatment, so I sucked it up and accepted the hit to my GPA.

Despite enjoying my educational dramatics, Dean was always my greatest cheerleader for my college pursuits. I ranted to him about the frustrations of different classes frequently, and I'd broken down due to the stress of an upcoming exam in front of him more than once. Every time, he let me get it all out without judgment. He never pressured me to finish talking quickly so we could get back to the music or other things that were more fun. Once I was drained, he would say something incredibly supportive. Like how what I was doing was a huge feat. Or how much he admired my commitment to my degree. He built me back up so I wanted to work harder and accomplish what I'd set out to achieve. To make him proud. Knowing he championed my dreams always seemed to give me the push I needed to complete the task.

At least he had in the past. I hoped last night hadn't ruined that.

God. My body was on edge today. One little thought of Dean in a completely innocent context made my skin tingle with excitement. Made my pulse increase and my palms sweat. Made me smile in a way I absolutely shouldn't be smiling. Made my cock hard in an instant. I fought the increasingly strong urge to jerk off to the memory, knowing that as good as it would be in the moment, the shame afterward would linger far longer.

Why had I let myself give in last night? It had made everything infinitely more complicated than the crush I had been harboring. It had made it real. His sounds. His kisses. The weight of his body. I had no idea how to act around him now. No idea how to go back to simply lusting after him in secret with no hope of my fantasies ever coming true.

My phone vibrated with a text, pulling me from my thoughts. I ignored it, struggling enough to focus on my academic reading without a second distraction. Glancing down at the page numbers in my textbook, I found I'd somehow flipped through five pages without registering anything. I had been scanning the words, but no comprehension had occurred. I sighed, pushed all thoughts of my best friend from my mind, and went back to the start of the chapter to read it over again.

Dean

ASH continued to avoid me for the next couple of days. At least as much as two people living in the same house could. It gave me a lot of time to think. I missed him. I missed our constant banter, the way he opened up to me and let me in. I wanted to go back to the way things were. Our friendship.

I also wanted more than that.

On the third day of Ash avoiding me, the Thorns got a group text from our band manager, Cory. He apparently had some news to share and wanted the four of us on a video call as soon as possible.

I made a cup of coffee in Ashy's fancyass machine before grabbing my laptop and settling on the couch for the call. Ash walked in a minute or two later with his own steaming mug. I patted the space next to me, figuring we might as well join the call together. He looked at the couch we had both been avoiding for days and frowned.

"Whatcha gonna do, Ashy? Buy a new sofa? Get your ass over here," I said, determined to try to get back to being regular Dean and Ash. It was only weird if we made it weird.

His shoulders fell, and he sighed, eventually joining me on the offending furniture. Still he left a good two feet between us, far more space than usual.

"So what'd you think this is about?" Ash asked before blowing across his coffee cup.

"Not sure. Last time Core met us like this was to tell us the 'Galaxies' dancers were joining us on tour. Maybe he's gonna tell us the next tour we'll get, like, a flying elephant or something?"

"An elephant…?" Ash shook his head at me.

"Bring on the whole damn circus I say. Gots to sell them tickets."

The familiar ring of a video call chimed out of the tinny speakers. Ash connected the call, and the faces of Carter, Beau, and Cory appeared. A wide smile immediately stretched across my cheeks. Even though we all got sick of each other after months on the road, I always missed the hell out of my band brothers after a few weeks of not seeing them.

"Friends!" I exclaimed, excitedly waving my hands in greeting.

"Oof," Ash grunted as my flailing arm accidently backhanded his shoulder.

I glanced at Ash and shot him an apologetic look.

"Hey, Deano. How you enjoying being home?" Carter asked.

"It's good. Good to see everyone. Ended up homeless there for a tick, but Papa Ashy came to the rescue and I'm staying with him."

"Oh, is he there with you? I can't see him," Carter said, leaning closer to the camera as if he was looking for Ash.

"Yup." Ash hesitated and then scooted over a few inches so some of him was in the frame. "Right here. Hi guys."

Another chorus of greetings rang out. While Ash was distracted with small talk, I shifted slightly closer and centered us both on the screen. I was careful to avoid our thighs touching, but being so near him—being able to smell him and sense his warmth radiating—was consuming my attention. Maybe he'd had the right idea to keep some distance between us on the couch.

"So." Cory took charge of the meeting, and we all quieted down like the good little children we were. "I know you're all set on taking a break through the summer. The label isn't crazy about it, but they respect it. However, a request has come in that I think you may be interested in. An easy gig—one day in Boston. It's a fundraiser for a struggling LGBTQ youth community center. They're looking for a band to play a concert. Sell some high-priced tickets and draw in some donations. They need to do some renos to prevent the place from being shut down. They're offering next to no money for the artist fee, but Thorns was their first choice to headline the event because you're all from the area and both Carter and Beau are out publicly."

Ash twitched beside me. Were Carter and Beau the only two LGBTQ members of the Thorns? I was beginning to wonder if I fell somewhere under that umbrella, though I had no idea which letter fit me. I didn't know where Ash stood, either, though I wished more than anything we could figure it out together.

Cory continued talking about the art classes and different programs Indigo House offered. Ash's thigh brushed against mine, making me tune out everything Cory said. I couldn't tell if Ash's move was intentional or a mistake. Optimistic that he was seeking reassurance, I pressed my own leg back into his, letting him know I was there for whatever form of support I could provide.

Eventually Cory finished his pitch. Obviously we were going to say yes. We all teased him incessantly, but beyond anyone in the industry, our manager has had our backs from day one. He wouldn't bother us by proposing bullshit, and he knew exactly what the Thorns wanted to stand for. The four of us wouldn't give a crap if we weren't getting paid for this.

"Fuck yes. I'm in," Carter said, used to being the spokesman for the group.

"Me too," Beau chimed in. "And so is Jamie if we do 'Galaxies' and want the dancers back."

Beau changed the angle of his webcam, and his boyfriend Jamie appeared next to him, grinning and nodding enthusiastically.

"Jam-Jam!" I waved at the appearance of my newest friend.

My stomach lurched as I recalled the last conversation I'd had with Jamie, when I had confessed I was attracted to Ash. I trusted Jamie not to say anything right now, but he wouldn't have mentioned our chat to Beau, would he? He said he wouldn't tell anyone. I hadn't thought about how his boyfriend factored into that promise.

I started babbling so nobody else could talk and potentially give away my secrets. "How are you, Jam-

Jam? Are things going well back at Juilliard? Did Hayden end up getting sent to that superfancy dance company? What's—"

"Dean!" Cory finally cut in. "Let's stay on topic at least until we've finalized a decision here."

Oops. Scolded for talking too much in class again.

"Sorry," I muttered. "But yes, I'm in."

"Great. Ash?" Cory asked.

"Um… yup. Yes. I'm in too," Ash stuttered awkwardly.

His leg was stiff against mine, his fingers white with tension, twisted together. I risked a glance at his face out of the corner of my eye. The guys probably couldn't see his clenched jaw on the screen, but Ash was clearly trying to mask his discomfort with this conversation.

Cory spun into logistics, which I couldn't have given less of a shit about. He would email us about it eventually. Or a car would show up someday to pick me up. Whatever. It's not like I had a lot of crap to pack. Could be ready in five minutes if I had to be.

Double-checking to make sure our lower halves were out of the frame, I took a risk and laid my hand on Ash's leg. I held my breath, silently hoping he wouldn't reject the gesture meant to comfort. The tension in his muscles seemed to relax with the contact. He released a long exhale, with just enough sound for me to hear. I took that as a good sign, but Ashy was a hard one to read. It was nearly impossible to know what he was thinking.

Ash

CONVERSATION continued on the call; however, all I could focus on was Dean's fingers on my thigh. They were moving now. His thumb slowly stroked the hemline of my cotton shorts, every so often catching a fraction of bare skin and causing an eruption of goose bumps. It was obviously intended to help me relax, but the caress was exhilarating.

I let him touch me, knowing it would lead nowhere good. Yet no part of me was stopping him.

Eventually Cory finished going over the logistics of the concert. I had a hard time concentrating, though from what I could gather, the foundation sounded even more fantastic the longer he went on. I completely supported the performance and the mission of the charity. The problem was that it hit so close to home right now. I couldn't help but be a little freaked out by the idea that someone was going to catch on to what had been going on in my head. Or what I had done with Dean.

After another minute or two of chatter, Cory excused himself from the call, and the four Thorns, plus Jamie, stuck around. Chase appeared in Carter's screen as well once the business was done. It was so nice to see both of my friends happy in their relationships. I looked down at Dean's hand on my knee. As right as it felt to have him touch me, there was no way it would ever be more than physical fun with him.

But maybe I could enjoy the physical for a while? Assuming he was interested in a repeat, that is.

"So we're not taking a fee for this, right?" Carter said once Cory disconnected, voicing the thought I'd had since Cory told us about the center. "We'll do the show for free?"

Moments like this made me love my band brothers more than ever. This wordless understanding between us. This *kinship*. They were the most thoughtful, good-hearted people I knew. How had I gotten so damn lucky?

Our artist fees had gotten ludicrous over the past few years. Performing one single concert made us all a lot of money. Even though we all loved playing, it was our job, and we had worked hard to charge as much as we did for performances and tickets. While the four of us didn't necessarily need the money as much anymore, there were people like Cory and our sound technicians who would still have to be paid regardless of whether the band took a check. In short, it cost *us* money to work for free.

We intentionally waited until Cory left the call to discuss the financials. Not charging for a show was a big

decision between the four of us that none of us would
voice to management until we were sure we were all on
the same page. We had only done it a handful of times,
and certainly not since we'd won our Grammy. But this
wasn't just any show. Even though I was nervous, this
was an important cause and something I was cautiously
eager to support.

I opened my mouth to agree with Carter.

"Absolutely," Dean said, jumping in before I could
speak. "Honestly, I'll probably make a donation too, or
try to help somehow. They sound like good people."

I had expected Dean to agree to doing the show
for free, but he'd still found a way to surprise me.
He smiled at me without any of the usual Phillips
cockiness. It was genuine and heartfelt. Lovely. I stared
at him, speechless.

"That's a good idea," Carter agreed, nodding,
oblivious to our moment.

"Yeah," I said. My throat was scratchy with
emotion. "That would be nice."

"Ashy, who was that new band you were texting
me about the other day?" Beau said. "The one with the
hot gay singer? Wonder if they would be interested in
opening for us?"

"Hey!" Jamie protested with an exaggerated pout.

"Sorry, babe," Beau said. "Obviously you're way
sexier." He laughed and kissed Jamie on the cheek.

"Um, also, what does that make me?" Carter asked.

"The not-hot gay singer," Dean confirmed
helpfully. "Pay attention."

Carter stuck out his tongue. Chase started to fawn
over Carter, defending his man from the humorous
attack. Goldfish had longer attention spans than the
Thorns did these days.

"The Keaton Stone Band," I responded to Beau's question over the other conversations. "They've got a couple cool tunes and are starting to gain some traction. From somewhere around here too, I think. They'd fit well with our vibe."

My answer appeared to go unnoticed. The two couples stared at each other on their respective screens, losing interest in everything else going on. Chase giggled at something Carter whispered in his ear. Beau nuzzled Jamie's neck. I rolled my eyes. Without a doubt the focus was gone from this meeting.

Dean chuckled at my reaction. "Jealous?" he asked under his breath.

I didn't dignify his comment with a response. Dean's devious fingers crept into the open leg of my shorts, teasing the sensitive skin there. The way he was touching me was far from scandalous, but it was enough to make it difficult to breathe. My cock went rock-hard in the thin cotton, and I fought the urge to squirm. Keeping our touches hidden while the other couples were blatantly doing the same thing was reckless... and unbelievably sexy.

What the hell was wrong with me?

"So, um, think we're gonna say goodbye now," Jamie said casually.

Beau snorted a laugh into Jamie's red hair.

"Maybe us too...?" Chase asked Carter suggestively.

"Oh fuck yes," Carter responded in a deeper-than-usual tone.

Gross. I *so* did not need to hear my friend's sex voice.

"Well, they's all gonna go screw like bunny rabbits. I guess that leaves you and me on our own, Ashy. What shall we do for the day?" Dean asked.

His words were playfully bantering for the benefit of our friends. His hands—*oh God, his hands*—were teasing me in a very nonjoking way.

Dean grinned at me innocently for the benefit of the camera. Nobody else on the planet could get away with the shit he did. Jamie shot us a funny look, but it was only for a fraction of a second before Beau distracted him again.

"Okay, byeee!" Chase made the decision for us all, and Carter chuckled as his window dropped out of the call.

The rest of us quickly said our goodbyes, and Dean slammed down the lid of his laptop.

"Well? What we gonna do, Ashy?" Dean asked again playfully.

I was so hard it hurt. The unforgiving cotton of my shorts had almost no stretch, and they had become excruciatingly tight. This was a bad decision. One I would surely regret as soon as the dust settled. Just like last time.

But I couldn't force myself to say no.

Ash

DEAN'S hands ghosted farther up my shorts. His eyes were locked on mine. As the seconds passed and I remained frozen, his gaze shifted from smoldering heat to tentative questioning. Again, it was so subtle that most people wouldn't have noticed a change. Only I wasn't most people when it came to Dean.

The pressure of his hand lessened an instant before his fingers began to withdraw from my thigh. Like he had lost his confidence and was going to back off. Before he could retreat completely, I grasped his hand and held it in place forcefully.

Yes, I was freaked out about this whole thing.

No, I wasn't about to stop.

Like last time, instinct took over and a calmness settled into me.

Dean looked down at my death grip on his hand and smirked. The cocky bastard fucking *winked* at me. Two could play at that game. As inexperienced as I was at this, I was *not* about to let him tease and torment me without giving him a taste of his own medicine. Dean and I were too competitive with each other for that. I had no doubt in my mind that his bedpost had a significant number of notches on it, but the last thing I was going to be was another mindless groupie stroking his ego. Boldly, I guided his hand upward until he was cupping my throbbing hard-on over my shorts. If nothing else, it was a test to see how he would react.

I closed my eyes in pleasure as he began lightly stroking his thumb back and forth over my cock. He was seemingly unbothered by the equipment I was packing, and the small amount of contact grew until he was caressing my full length steadily. The intimate touch shot bolts of lightning through my body until I was reduced to gasps and whimpers. I fisted the thin fabric of his shirt, desperate for something to hold on to. My head was a mess with want and desire and confusion. Then his lips found my neck, nuzzling upward until his tongue licked over the shell of my ear. Suddenly nothing else mattered.

His mouth distracted me while his sneaky fingers moved to unfasten the button of my shorts. I pulled Dean's T-shirt over his head quickly before shucking my own. His skin was scorching hot as I stroked over his collarbone, down the planes of his smooth chest. Across his tattoos.

I traced along every drawing, most of which I'd been there for while it was being inked. Each had a story. Each was intrinsically Dean. On his left triceps was the freehand sketch of Carter's childhood home, the cover art for Thorns's first album. On his right forearm was a bass guitar with the strings arranged into a heartbeat line. Down his chest was a photorealistic image of Amberwood's clock tower, a rickety hundred-year-old structure that stood directly across from the diner. Along his lowest rib was the word "home" in his mother's flourishing cursive. Dean didn't start getting tattoos until a few years ago. Despite his general lackadaisical attitude, he hadn't wanted to chance it with cheap ink or hasty decisions. I loved his tattoos almost as much as I loved my own.

Dean was firm and masculine; I grew exponentially more turned on the more I explored his body. It had never, *ever* been like this with a woman. Not once had I been filled with so much want before. So much lust. I was beginning to understand the immense appeal of sex. If nothing else, this experiment had helped me put a label on my own sexuality.

I only hoped I didn't lose my best friend in the process.

Dean's strong hands lifted my hips so he could shove my shorts and underwear down. I fought the urge to cover myself up. I felt exposed. Far more so than the last time Dean had seen me naked. Dean shifted off the couch, spread my thighs, and knelt between them. My mouth dropped open. It was the most erotic moment of my life; I knew I would fantasize about that image for years to come.

Not at all tentatively, Dean kissed his way up the sensitive skin of my left thigh, setting fire to nerves that were already on edge. He licked down my hip joint, a move that was so effortlessly sexy I couldn't help but groan. I ran my fingers through his curly locks, pushing the ringlets back so I could meet his gaze. God, I'd thought about doing that for so long. Dean looked up at me, his eyes sparkling, his smile easy and relaxed. He was so damn beautiful. How had it taken me this long to notice him?

Ever since we'd met, Dean had never been predictable. He constantly found ways to catch me off guard. He did stupid little things to make me laugh. Make me roll my eyes. More recently, make my heart flutter.

When Dean started touching me, I didn't know where he planned to take this encounter. I figured maybe he was planning something similar to what had happened last time, or maybe at most we would use our hands on each other. Even though his actions appeared to be moving in this direction, I still gasped in surprise when Dean took my cock between his soft lips.

His mouth was perfect. Warm. Wet. Tight. The suction he was using, coupled with the constant stroking of his tongue, made it seem like he had done this before. Maybe he had. Not long ago I would have assumed I knew all the highlights of Dean's sex life; I had no idea anymore. He gagged when he tried to take me too deep and then backed off a little. I rested my hand under his chin, encouraging him to look up at me. His eyes were watery but bright and energetic. Using his hand to cover the last few inches, he took me back into his mouth.

It was hard to tell if it was because of his skill or because I had secretly fantasized about Dean for so long, but it was undoubtedly the best blowjob I'd ever had. For months now when I had been alone at night, I had imagined this, ultimately knowing it would never happen. My conscience had nagged me for days afterward for even dreaming about it. Now that it was a reality, my wildest imaginings didn't compare.

Dean kept me on the precipice. I was heartbeats away from giving into the ultimate pleasure; only my unwillingness for this perfect moment to be over pulled me back from the edge. He licked and he sucked and he was so damn vulnerable that I lost all track of time and my surroundings. It might have lasted a minute. It might have lasted an hour. A whole damn marching band could have paraded through the house and I wouldn't have noticed.

All that mattered was Dean.

I had no idea what was to come in the future for us— we were already on borrowed time—so I did everything in my power to drink in the moment. The way his stupidly sexy curls refused to stay out of his eyes. The way his naked, toned chest rose and fell quickly with exertion. The sensation of his stubble scraping against the delicate skin of my thighs. Everywhere he touched me became an erogenous zone. Every lap of his tongue drew a new moan from my throat. Dean cupped my balls at the same moment that he circled the head of my cock, and the combination was all too much.

My eyes flew wide. "Oh fuck, I'm gonna—"

I frantically tried to pull him off me, unable to imagine a scenario where my straight friend would want me to come in his mouth. My cock popped free, and I barely registered the confused look on Dean's face before the first shot hit his neck. He kept hold of my cock with one hand, stroking me through my orgasm, seemingly unbothered by the mess.

When my pulse began to return to normal, I looked at the picture in front of me. Dean's face, neck, and torso were covered with streaks of my come. His lips were puffy and swollen. His hair was a mess from my fingers. I had thought Dean merely on his knees was the hottest visual ever, but this utterly debauched look was in a category of its own.

Dean's eyes were glazed over, his reactions slow as I finally cleared my throat to speak again.

"Holy shit" was all I could muster.

"Yeah," he agreed, voice a little shaken and gravelly.

I wanted to get him off too, but I would need a sec because my brain and my body weren't functioning at the moment. We stared at each other in silence as I floated back down to Earth.

I shook my head in disbelief at what had just transpired. "How the fuck were you so good at that?"

Dean

PICKING up my shirt to wipe the dripping come from my body, I forced myself to chuckle at Ash's dumbfounded words. The sound was awkward in my ears, barely audible over my rapidly thumping heart.

For once I didn't want to laugh or make a stupid joke. Didn't want to wipe this moment away with an old T-shirt. I wanted to savor the feeling of rightness that washed over me when I was on my knees for him. To tell him that even though I'd never given a blowjob before, having him in my mouth was the most natural sex of my life. Wanted to tell him how much I wished he'd have let me swallow his come: "I was good at it because I can read you like a book I've read a thousand times." I wanted to say, "I know all of your tells, your body language, what your reactions mean. I know you better than anyone. Better than I know myself most days."

"I'm good at everything, Ashy. You should know that by now," I told him instead.

My words made me cringe internally.

It was easier to make a lighthearted remark. To throw away the intensity of what happened with a typical Deanism. Reduce the risk of Ash panicking like he had last time. To be what he expected me to be. What everyone expected me to be.

"Come here," he said.

I fought the shakes and shudders that threatened the stability of my knees. With his hands on my waist, I stood in front of him. His gentle fingers slipped down my belly. I flexed my muscles under his caress, knowing Ash wouldn't care that I hadn't been putting in my hours at the gym. I wanted to look good for him nonetheless. My dick was stone in my pants, turned on beyond description from what had just transpired. I was sure that if Ash simply looked at me in the right way, I would explode.

Ash ran the back of his hand over my length. I bit into my lower lip to stop myself from crying out. He popped open the button of my pants and slid them down over my hips.

"Do you *ever* wear underwear?" he teased me with a smirk.

I opened my mouth to make a smartass remark, but Ash chose that moment to close his fingers around my cock.

"Fuuuck," I groaned.

His grip was loose. Hesitant. If it had been anybody other than Ash the hold barely would have affected me. But everything with Ash was on a heightened plane.

Ash's strokes grew in confidence. He used his other hand to explore my balls. My hips. My ass. I'd never thought much about anything other than my cock being sexual—for so many years sex had been about getting off quickly before heading back to the tour bus—but the way Ash was touching me made me curious for more.

He caressed my body lightly. It was a different touch than I expected from his large, calloused musician's hands. But it was so *Ash*. Selfless. The caretaker. He looked at me with a shaky smile. The uncertainty in his eyes undid me: the earnestness and desire to please. It was a look that gave me hope. In the fleeting moment, I wondered if maybe, just maybe, despite what he'd said last time, he might feel the same way I did.

"Oh God," I stuttered as he swiped over the sensitive head of my cock with his thumb.

Using my reaction to his advantage, Ash continued to torment the spot again and again. My body strained; the muscles in my ass and legs began to shake harder with tension. Ash's left hand stilled on my hip, steadying me and gripping tight enough to bruise.

Color flashed across my squeezed-shut eyelids. Every thought evaporated from my mind as my body erupted in pleasure. My knees buckled, and Ash's strong arms caught my dead weight before I collapsed. I must have been making noise, because my throat was raw. Ash guided me to sit down on the couch as I caught my breath.

I blinked as the world began to come back into focus. Ash was cleaning up with my already-soiled T-shirt. I was completely relaxed and shot him a lazy smile.

"Hey," I greeted him.

"Hey," he teased back.

I patted the couch next to me, encouraging him to move closer. He threw the shirt on the floor and followed my gesture. Staring into his eyes, I looked for any trace of uncertainty or sign that he was going to crash again. Finding none, I took a risk and ran my fingers over his cheek before leaning in to kiss him softly on the lips.

"Dean, I—" Ash started. I cut him off with another kiss before he could give a logical reason why this was a bad idea or why it shouldn't happen again. Maybe it was naïve, but I wanted to live in the postorgasmic glow for a few more minutes.

"Let's have a lazy day today," I suggested. "We can watch dumb movies and eat crap and not worry about anything else."

I grabbed the remote off the coffee table and turned the TV on before he had a chance to protest.

Ash sucked in air like he was going to give some big response, but then he just nodded. "Okay."

Ash

Three Months Earlier. Leeds, United Kingdom

"ASHY, you coming out tonight? I heard about this club, man, the girls there are smokin' hot." Dean waggled his eyebrows playfully as he tuned his bass.

My stomach sank like it did every time Dean encouraged me to come out with him these days. The darkness of the backstage area hid my grimace. We were five minutes away from going onstage, and the din of the excited crowd was audible from the wings. Dean's invites were well-intentioned, and in the past I would have likely joined him in whatever shenanigans he suggested. But things had changed between us recently. They had begun to change even before that fateful night at the *Grammys*.

I schooled my expression for his benefit.

"Nah, I think I'll pass tonight. Too tired."

"You're *always* too tired these days!" Dean pouted. "It's bad enough these boring buckets are all practically married. What's the point of all this without the... adoring fans?"

Carter scoffed in the background at the insult. I rolled my eyes at my best friend.

"You mean the fans out there?" I gestured to the packed house in front of us. "I'd rather give them a good show for the money they paid instead of fucking my way through England and falling asleep at my drums."

"Judgy, judgy," Dean scolded. "Come on, Ashy! We're young. We're far away from home. We're in a fucking band! When you're ninety years old and have saggy balls and a carpet of back hair you're gonna regret not doing what you wanted when you had the opportunity."

I stared at him, knowing he was baiting me and not wanting to engage two minutes before we went onstage. The comment stung, however. It hit something deep inside of me that knew that in a weird way, Dean was right. I didn't want to regret not doing what I wanted. But what I wanted to do wasn't something I could voice to Dean.

Our intro music began. Carter jumped up and down twice—his preshow ritual—before running onstage. The crowd went mental, screaming and cheering as they got their first glance of our star. We followed him and my brain went into autopilot. No more time for thinking, for questioning, for overanalyzing. Game face on.

Present Day

THE memory of what had happened in Leeds hit me as I stood in the dark, staring at the sofa responsible for all my recent transgressions.

Dean and I had hung out all afternoon. We stayed far enough apart to not exactly be cuddling, but neither of us seemed particularly concerned when our bodies accidently came into contact either. Whenever one of us got up—to accept the pizza delivery or use the bathroom—we came back to nearly the identical position. It was comfortable. Normal. It was as close to a perfect day as I could imagine, even though I was 99 percent sure he was only acting this way to avoid having a real conversation.

When the sun sank lower in the sky, I knew I should call it a night before we accidently fell asleep together again. Dean headed up to his room while I shut off all the lights. Grabbing Dean's crusty, come-soaked T-shirt off the floor, I was now left alone with my guilty thoughts.

Dean and I were somewhere in this zone between the best friends we always had been and something completely new. I wasn't sure what, exactly; however, hooking up twice wasn't as easy to write off as getting caught up in the moment the first time.

He'd had my dick in his mouth, for Christ's sake.

What I'd been afraid to want for so long was finally coming to a juncture that seemed more impossible to ignore with each passing day. The intensity of our European tour had provided little opportunity to slow down and sit with myself. Now that it was just Dean and me in the quiet of my house in our sleepy town, thoughts of him consumed my every breath.

I had wrestled with this growing attraction to Dean for so long. Since before the *Grammys*, when the hookup with Maddy made everything real. Since the night in Leeds that had nothing, and everything, to do with him. My personal life was usually pretty simple.

I was used to being the reliable one. The boring one who faded into the background. Papa Ash. Somehow everything in my world had become a secret.

Dean and I needed to talk. I knew that the outcome of the conversation was likely to hurt me. But I couldn't conjure an ounce of regret over getting to hang out with him so simply this afternoon. Delaying the inevitable.

I shook my head, bringing myself back into the moment. The living room. The delinquent furniture.

"Gotta burn this fucking couch," I muttered to myself before heading upstairs to bed.

Ash

THE next morning I woke early to the incessant tapping of the woodpecker that had made a home in the tree outside my window. I was used to the sounds of the city and the road. Wildlife, not so much. Grumbling, I flung the pillow over my head to try to drown out the noise, until I realized it was a lost cause. I was wide-awake.

I threw on some basketball shorts and a sleeveless T-shirt, deciding I would make use of the cool morning and go for a run. After locking the front door behind me, I stretched lightly to warm up my muscles before taking off at a jog down my driveway. The steady thump of my legs relaxed me as the world slowed down and I let my mind wander. I made my way around the small lake adjoining my property. It would be busy with families later in the day, but for now I had the trails to myself.

By the time I got back home an hour later, the unsettled energy was gone, and my body felt accomplished. It was a new day. I was an adult, and I could handle this.

How, exactly, I had no idea. But I could *totally* handle this.

I showered quickly to wash off the grime before heading to the kitchen to make myself some breakfast. I had just filled a mug with fresh-made coffee when I noticed movement outside on the deck. It was unusual for Dean to be up this early, but he had his laptop in front of him and was making wild gestures and talking to himself enthusiastically. As I pulled back the screen door, he smiled at me and held up his hand in a silent greeting before gesturing to the cell phone at his ear.

"Yeah, yeah, that sounds great. I'll be there. Thanks so much. Looking forward to it. Okay, bye," Dean said into the phone before disconnecting the call. His eyes sparkled in the morning light as he tapped something into his phone and then set it down on the patio table.

"You're up early," I commented, blowing across the rim of my coffee mug.

"Yeah, couldn't sleep last night and wanted to get a jump on things this morning."

Dean focused on his computer screen, reading and scrolling through whatever had captured his attention. I'd hoped to have a chance to talk today about what had gone down between us last night, but whenever Dean got this enthralled with something it was hard to have a conversation with him about anything else.

"Get a jump on what exactly?" I asked, trying to resist sneaking a peak at what he was looking at on the laptop screen.

"The youth center Cory told us about. Kept thinking last night that there was more I should do. That was the director, Jasmine, on the phone. I'm gonna drive up there tomorrow to meet her."

"Oh?" I said, taken aback by Dean's answer. "I didn't know you were interested in that kinda thing."

"Thought it might be nice to give back now that I've got some time. Low-income families and whatnot. Plus LGBTQ stuff. Not sure what I can do exactly. Maybe a music program of some kind. Jasmine and I are gonna figure it out when I'm there."

Dean's words were casual, but there was a surprising amount of thought behind them. My mouth fell agape as I fought to formulate a response. Honestly I was a little blown away. Dean wasn't exactly known for his selflessness. On the other hand, his reasoning made perfect sense. He had grown up in a single-parent family, and while he never spoke about his financial situation growing up, he was always on the school-sponsored meal plans. I knew that the family was never well-off, but Cherie always did her best for Dean and his sisters. It was entirely possible things were harder for them than any of the Phillipses had ever let on.

My mind also snagged on his LGBTQ comment. What exactly did he mean by that?

"You wouldn't mention…?" I waved my hand between us, hoping he would get the gist.

He tilted his head to the side, shooting me a look that was equal parts sarcastic and insulted.

"Come on, Ashy. You know me better than that. What happened between us is none of anyone's business but our own."

"I know," I said quickly, nodding like it was obvious.

I did know. I believed him. Although Dean had a habit of speaking before he thought, I trusted his discretion about the important things. This situation was beyond weird, and I had no idea how I felt about it yet. The possibility of anyone else finding out—no matter how unlikely—made me squirmy.

Dean

DRIVING down the freeway, I was singing along to every song that came on the radio at the top of my lungs. Lyrics? Who cared what they were supposed to be? The ones I made up were way better anyway. The guys should absolutely let me write more songs for the band.

As the traffic increased, I followed the directions from the built-in GPS while I grew closer to the core of the city. Ever since Cory told us about Indigo House, I hadn't been able to stop thinking about it. I wanted to help more than by playing a few songs at the fundraiser. It was also a good excuse to spend a few hours away from Ash today; might give him an opportunity to think things through before I pressed for a conversation. Yes, I was undeniably procrastinating, but I knew Ash like the back of my hand. Ash needed time to adjust to any new idea, and I wanted to give him that.

Plus I was terrified.

I turned onto the street the center was on and located the address, somehow finding a parking spot right out front. Stepping inside the building, I immediately saw why this place needed help. There was a small reception desk at the front and a large lounge area over to the left. The room was covered in old wallpaper, which was faded and peeling at the top. There were a bunch of couches and chairs—a disarray of colors, fabrics, and styles—that had all seen better days. The windows were large but dirty. The carpet was thin. A few teenagers were scattered throughout; the energy was low and all of them were sitting by themselves, intent on their phones. Overall the room had good bones. It just needed some funding and some love.

"Hello, welcome to Indigo House," the perky receptionist said.

"Hi there. I'm Dean Phillips. I have a meeting with Jasmine?"

"Sure. Make yourself at home and I'll grab her for you."

A minute or two later, an attractive young woman with bright blue hair and a vintage 1950s style dress came around the corner.

"Dean? Hey, I'm Jasmine Callaghan. I'm the director here at Indigo House. Thanks so much for making the time to visit."

"Hey, nice to meet you." I reached out to shake her hand. "Thanks for inviting me."

"I must admit, I was pretty surprised when you called. I'm kinda a huge fan, and I'm super nervous right now." She had a wide smile on her face and giggled bashfully. It was a look I recognized, as I got that a lot from groupies. It was a look that had gotten me into trouble more times than I could count.

Ash's face popped into my mind, and a pang of discomfort ran through me. Not that I had done anything wrong. Was this what guilt felt like? I made a conscious effort to keep my tone purely professional and not include any of the flirt I may have sometimes included with fans.

I laughed with her, trying to hide the awkwardness of my thoughts.

"No need to be nervous. Like I said on the phone, our manager was telling us about this place, and I just wanted to do more, you know?"

"Yeah, I get it. I've been here for ten years—a volunteer before I became paid staff—and I still always think there's more I should do. Why don't I show you around, and then we can chat about ways to get involved?"

I nodded and followed Jasmine as she took me through the building. The other rooms were all in similar shape to the lobby. She talked enthusiastically about the different programs Indigo House ran and what they wanted to do if the fundraising efforts were successful. Her dedication to the place was evident, and her eagerness was contagious. I was even more committed to helping after listening to her talk.

We finished the tour in Jasmine's small office. I glanced around at all the personal touches in the dingy space. Drawings lined the walls, likely from the center's participants. Brightly colored coffee mugs and knickknacks took over the small desk. A photo frame on the window ledge surrounded a shot of a beautiful golden retriever.

"So," Jasmine said, pulling my attention away from my examination of her life, "tell me a little about what you were thinking."

Taking a breath, I wasn't quite sure where to start. I was a dumb rock star. I had little to contribute compared to the miracles she worked here.

"Well, I grew up in a single-parent home. We were luckier than a lot of people, but sometimes seeing the other kids with all their afterschool activities that we couldn't afford was tough." I paused.

It wasn't a horrible sob story by any stretch of the imagination. We were never hungry and we always had a roof over our heads, but I had realized over the last few years exactly how difficult things must have been for my mom sometimes.

Jasmine nodded her head reassuringly, and so I continued. "I kinda talked my way into joining the Thorns when we were back in high school, but I'd wanted to learn to play music for years before that. Lessons cost money. It's crazy to think how different my life would be if I hadn't had that lucky break, ya know? Who knows how many Picassos or Madonnas never become anybody because they can't afford the lessons? Because they never have the opportunity or nobody ever tells them they can."

"I agree completely," Jasmine said. "And even if they're not going to be 'Picassos or Madonnas'— as you say—the self-confidence from learning a new skill and meeting other LGBTQ+ kids is tremendously important."

"Exactly," I agreed.

"We've never had a real music program here," Jasmine said, clicking her pen thoughtfully. "Honestly it's mostly a funding problem. We do visual art because paintbrushes and paper cost less than guitars and pianos. But I know a couple of the regular kids would go crazy for music classes."

"Cost isn't an issue," I said quickly.

I had enough connections that I could surely get the beginner instruments they needed donated to Indigo House. And if for some reason I couldn't, I would cover the cost myself.

"We'd need to hire a regular teacher, but maybe a workshop or two with a high-profile musician would help get the word out in the beginning?" Jasmine suggested, looking at me expectantly.

I chuckled at the concept of some poor kid trying to learn anything from me. "I want to be involved, but I can barely play the bass, and I'd be the worst teacher in the world."

She laughed at my self-deprecating comment.

"But fortunately for you," I continued, "I know the perfect guy for the job."

Ash

"YOU want me to do what?" I asked Dean after he got home from his meeting in Boston.

Sneaky bastard got me all buttered up too. Played me like a fucking fiddle. First he came home all flirty and affectionate. Handed off the homemade brownies from the diner that he *knows* are my number one ultimate weakness. Poured me a glass of wine, gave me a little shoulder massage. Then he sprang teaching music classes at Indigo House on me.

The whole thing was baffling to me because *I know him*. I know his tricks and how he smiles and bats his eyelashes and gets his way. I mean, yeah, I normally go along with it—and obviously I was going to agree to the music classes too—but I didn't even *notice* he was playing me this time. He kissed me sweetly and rubbed my back, and I was so fucking cartoon-heart eyes about him I never even *noticed* what he was doing.

Fucking hell. I was in so much trouble.

"Come on, Ashy. Pleaaase? This place could be so good for those kids, and you play, like, fifty different instruments. You taught me how to play the bass, remember?"

"That was different." I sighed. "You were trying to be a drummer, and I almost got knocked unconscious by your sticks, like, three times."

"Yeah, I never did get those twirls right, huh?"

"I don't know why you insisted on trying to do fancy spins before even being able to play the fucking drums, but whatever."

"Cause the twirls are the best part of being a drummer!"

"Only when you're actually a drummer first."

"I was basically there. Smack the thingy on the second and fourth beat, crash the cymbals as loud as possible. Easy peasy."

"I think we got off topic." I rubbed my temples, trying to remember what the point of this conversation was.

Dean came up behind the chair I was sitting in and started running his fingers through my hair.

"The important thing was that you taught me to play," he said.

After a minute I relaxed into his touch, sighing in contentment.

"You did," Dean continued, more softly this time. He returned to the chair beside me, pulling it closer than before. "I had no idea what I was doing, but I wanted to hang out with you and Carter and Beau so badly. You spent every evening in the diner with me, repeating the chords over and over when I couldn't get them right. I'm sure you had a million other things you could have been doing and that I made you crazy. But you never complained. Just kept working with me until it finally clicked."

He had grabbed my hand partway through his speech. Dean's thoughtfulness was generally buried under bravado. Under selfishness and showmanship and the undying need to be the center of attention. However, in moments like this, it was evident how much he had the ability to care. He showed that side of himself to very few people. It made my feelings for him so much more complicated.

I remembered those nights at the diner vividly. My mom kept threatening to ground me for neglecting my homework and my violin. I never told her what I was up to or who I was with. Teaching Dean to play somehow felt too important to argue with her over. It all worked out in the end, though. Dean was never going to be the world's best musician, but Thorns wouldn't be the same without him. I certainly wouldn't be the same without him.

"Come here." I leaned in to take his soft lips, needing the connection between us.

I wasn't sure if it was the right thing to do. I just knew I couldn't resist.

We kissed and got lost in each other, hands tracing skin, breath mingling as one. Eventually the need to take things further won out. I led Dean upstairs and into my bedroom for the first time. It was purposeful and thought-out. Calculated. Beautiful. He spent the night with me in my bed. In my arms. It wasn't some spontaneous romp in the living room anymore. It was so much more than that. I stopped worrying. Everything about this was right.

Fuck the couch.

Ash

Three Months Earlier. Leeds, United Kingdom

MY heartbeat raced faster, matching the low thumping of the music from the club as I nervously sipped my drink in a dark corner. Our concert in Leeds hadn't even been over for half an hour when I slipped away before the stagehands had finished dismantling our setup, before Dean could beg me to play wingman for him again. Or worse, ask too many questions about where I was headed.

I scanned the dim room, the smell of alcohol and cologne pungent in the air. The vibration of the bass was so deep it made my teeth throb. Swaying bodies moved together as one collective, each individual attempting to stand out, but ultimately contributing to the anonymous blob of sweat and skin and sex. The partygoers' intentions were no different here than at the club I'd refused to go to with Dean. The drinking and dancing and laughter were identical. Locals looking for an opportunity to blow off some steam on a Saturday night. There was only one difference at this particular rave.

All of the visitants were male.

Bare chests and toned abs glistened under the technicolor lights as bodies fluttered and rolled. A herd of egotistical peacocks showing off, petitioning for the attention of a prospective mate. One particularly bright specimen met my gaze and winked at me. The allure had merit, but all flashy Cinderellas returned to regular garb the morning after the ball.

I fought to be impartial. To do what I set out here tonight to accomplish. To see if it was only one Dean Phillips who turned my head or if there was another—*safer*—masculine option to explore. I didn't want to be here—not really. I was exhausted from months on the road, and a late-night meat market had little appeal. I wanted a partner, not a one-night stand. But I was tired of living in my head. Tired of second-guessing, of not knowing for sure.

"Hey." A guy appeared next to me, taking a drink of whatever was in his glass.

The guy was fortunately fully clothed, as I was still working up the nerve to jump into the fray. He was shorter than me, as most people were. It was hard to tell the exact color in the lighting, but he had short dark hair and wore a button-up shirt. Objectively he was attractive, yet there was nothing about him that particularly stood out.

No slightly too-long, ridiculous curls that begged for my fingers to run through them.

"Hey," I responded politely.

His gaze shamelessly slid down my body. A lick of heat curled in my belly. The exchange wasn't urgent or momentous but definitely made my pulse race in a way it hadn't with any woman recently. Interesting.

"I'm Ben," he said, shaking my hand.

"Um, Alex." I tried to hide the stutter over my lie.

I waited to see if there was any sign he recognized me. My face wasn't as easily noticed in a crowd as Carter's or Dean's, but the last thing I wanted tonight was for a fan to spot me here and start asking questions. Fortunately, Ben didn't appear to know who I was.

"So, Alex," he purred, "wanna dance?" He reached over and touched me on the hip suggestively.

His hand burned into me; that small mundane amount of contact made everything real. For most people it would mean next to nothing. A simple touch. An invitation. It was only the second time a guy had touched me like that. And the first had been an accident.

The image of Dean's rough hand on my thigh when we were in bed with Maddy was seared into my long-term memory. The incidental contact had somehow become the most meaningful sexual experience of my life to date. *How fucking sad was that?* It was my unfailing fantasy these days when it was just me alone at night. Ben's small graceful hand on my hip was nothing like the calloused musician's hand that consumed my fantasies. That haunted my dreams.

But nothing would ever happen with Dean. I needed to let that go. That's why I'd come here tonight.

I nodded to the real live man in front of me with renewed determination. "Yeah, let's dance."

Ash

SUNDAY came around quickly enough, and Dean and I made our way to his mom's for our standing brunch invitation. It wasn't a long drive from my place to Cherie's house. Nothing was too far in Amberwood, I supposed.

When we arrived and let ourselves in, it was a shock to see my parents standing around the kitchen counter chatting with Cherie. The three of them had become friendly in the years since we had formed the Thorns, though I wouldn't necessarily have expected them to be the type of acquaintances who brunched together. Then again, Cherie's weekly brunches were notorious for including anyone and everyone she saw fit to invite, so perhaps I shouldn't have been surprised. She was a typical Phillips after all. Catching me off guard was their specialty.

The whole thing was incredibly domestic. We sat around Cherie's table—which dominated most of the footprint of the small dining room—eating sausages and tomatoes and three types of eggs. Dean and I sat next to each other at one end, joking about being relegated to the "kids table." He told our parents about Indigo House and the idea for the music program. I thought my mom's eyes were going to pop out of her head with surprise and excitement at the idea. Despite my trepidation in high school about telling her I was teaching Dean to play the bass—which was more due to the impact on my own schooling than anything else— my mom was a lifelong advocate for music education. She immediately made the offer to become involved in some way, to bring some of her friends from the symphony on board. Dean, of course, was delighted, and I got to see him in action, pitching different ideas for their involvement. I tried to contain the look of pride in my eyes as Dean spoke, knowing that if any of our three parents noticed how I was looking at him, there would be questions.

"So what's it like being back in Amberwood?" Dad asked once the food was mostly eaten. "Must seem small compared to Paris and London."

His teasing smile made me laugh. Dad had always made his affinity for Amberwood known. He was one of the lucky few to have a big-city job but a small-town life. In his younger years, he'd been a guest violinist with some of the largest symphonies in Europe. All the prestige in the world hadn't meant much to him. He only ever wanted to play with the Boston Symphony and live in our weird little town. Raise a family.

"It's good. Nice to finally have a chance to live in my own house for a bit," I said.

"And things are going well between you two boys? Staying together?" Mom added with a worried tone. "No arguments?"

"No, ma'am," Dean answered. "We've been getting along reeeal good these days."

I stuttered around the bite of food I was eating, sending me into a very not-subtle coughing fit. Dean chuckled beside me, covering his laugh with a sip of his orange juice. My outburst caused a few funny looks, but mercifully nobody remarked on Dean's suggestive tone. Dean's humor went over my parents' heads most of the time; they just thought he was strange. Usually we both got a kick out of their reactions to him.

"Careful you don't choke on the sausage, Ashy," Dean whispered so only I could hear once I got my breathing back under control.

I kicked him under the table.

The rest of the meal went on less dramatically. It was kind of nice to see our worlds colliding. Cherie meant everything to Dean. They had a bond unlike any other parent-son relationship I'd seen in my life. There was no topic off-limits, no subject left untouched. I felt awful knowing Dean was hiding something from his mom because of me; I knew it went against everything he was.

On the way home—car loaded up with leftovers—I listened to Dean happily singing along off-key to the radio. Making up his own lyrics, as always. I shook my head, smiling at the ridiculous simplicity of the moment. Two of the members of the biggest rock band on the planet. Tupperware containers of sliced ham and blueberry muffins in the back seat. Windows down and hearts full from time with family. No pretension. No expectations.

I inhaled serenely and joined in with the harmonies.

Dean

IT took a surprisingly short amount of time for things to begin coming together with the music program. As grumbly as Ash was to begin with, he and I were knocking items off the to-do list at a breakneck pace. We worked well together. We always had, but something about this was different. Ash seemed to innately know how to plan this project, and I was good at promotion and sweet-talking local businesses into donating goods.

We'd even come up with a name for the program: Heartbeat. Ash and I both played tempo-driven instruments in the Thorns, and so the name fit on a couple of levels. We would teach a few classes leading up to the big concert, while we were still in town, and then Jasmine would find a local instructor to take over on a more regular basis. Ash's mom even contributed by suggesting a few names of local music instructors she knew. Indigo House was so excited about the whole thing that they decided to convert one of their common areas into a music space in the renovation designs.

Jasmine was a wonderful advocate for the project. She was always around to lend a hand with whatever I needed, often bringing me coffee or offering to stay late. It didn't hurt that occasionally she would bring her beautiful golden retriever, Bella, along for break-time snuggles.

Despite all her efforts, Ash constantly seemed on edge around Jasmine. I couldn't figure out why Ash didn't seem to like her when Jasmine was going so far out of her way to help.

A pleasant exhaustion overtook me as the weeks trickled by. Ash and I had developed somewhat of a routine, driving to Indigo House or working at the kitchen table each afternoon. Making dinner together or grabbing something quick on the way home. Falling into his bed every night.

I wasn't really sure what had changed, how Ash and I had gone from hooking up a couple of times to whatever was going on now. Our single-minded focus on Heartbeat left little energy for intense conversations about anything else. After the first night he'd pulled me into his bedroom, I never seemed to leave. The first few nights were a little awkward, with one or the other of us making up some excuse as to why it made more sense to share a bed. As the days went on, questions stopped being raised, and we simply both made our way to Ash's room each night. A lot of the time we were too beat to get up to anything sexy, but having his solid body next to mine helped me to sleep better than I had in years.

Neither of us seemed inclined to instigate a conversation about what was happening. The walls of his house became our safe space, where we could just *be*. We sat a little closer on the couch when we watched sports. He found ways to touch me as we worked side-by-side in the kitchen. I kissed him good morning, good night, and dozens of other times throughout the day. He got much more comfortable with sex, initiating it almost as often as I did. We explored each other's bodies and learned what we liked together.

This felt like the best version of dating. Comfortable. Easygoing. We didn't take ourselves too seriously, and there was no pretense of going out of our way to impress each other. I had a habit of leaving my clothes scattered around the floor. He hated doing the dishes. We were messy in our separate ways and acknowledged our own flaws. Because of that, we worked well together as roommates, which I learned was a valuable and underrated trait in a romantic relationship.

But in the rare moments when I found myself alone—after Ash had drifted off to sleep or when he was busy studying—my thoughts sometimes spiraled. How long could this thing between us last? Did Ash feel the same way I did?

Was this all a gigantic mistake?

Not only had I never had a relationship before, I had never even *considered* being in one. I'd watched my mom and sister struggle with romances for most of my life. Being part of a couple was a lot of damn work. A lot of unnecessary drama. A lot of frustration and disappointment and ultimately, heartbreak.

What I had with Ash was the opposite of all those things. Being with him was *so* fucking easy.

Was that a bad thing?

Were we doing it wrong?

If we talked more—acknowledged what was happening between us—would Ash admit he wanted this to work as badly as I did? Or would he panic again and put a stop to us once and for all?

Ash had been the best part of my life for as long as I could remember. I refused to lose him. Sticking my head in the sand and ignoring the situation was far safer.

The night before the first music class, Ash and I were sitting up in his bed together as usual. His back was propped up against the headboard. He was wearing his reading glasses—when had glasses ever been so hot before?—cramming for a final exam in one of the college courses he was taking. Tired of overthinking in the silence, I gave up pretending to look at my phone and set it on my nightstand.

"I forgot to tell you, Jasmine said the funniest thing today." I proceeded to tell Ash the hilarious story about Bella and a neighborhood squirrel.

By the time I got to the end, I was snorting with laughter, but Ash remained silent, wearing only the smallest of smiles. His dimple wasn't even showing.

"What? Why aren't you laughing?" I finally asked.

"I am. It was a cute story." Ash took off his glasses and folded them up.

I looked at him skeptically, trying to figure out what his deal was.

"A lot of your stories these days are about her," Ash added. He was trying to be casual, but I didn't buy it.

"About Bella?" I asked, knowing full well that wasn't what he meant but unsure where he was going with this.

Ash rolled his eyes. "About *Jasmine*."

I struggled to understand the issue, so like usual, I tried to get a laugh.

"What's wrong, Ashy?" I cooed at him, running my hands playfully up his bare chest. "You jealous?"

I was only teasing, but Ash scoffed loudly and crossed his arms. It finally clicked as to why he had been so cranky around Jasmine the past few weeks. Ash actually *was* jealous!

"I am *not* jealous of Jasmine," Ash said.

He totally was.

I had started this conversation as a way to make myself less anxious about us, but somehow, in a few minutes, it had gone sideways.

Maybe I was even worse at this than I thought.

I considered the situation objectively. Jealous Papa Ash was seriously adorable, but I didn't want to cause a stupid, unfounded argument over something that wasn't real. Didn't want to make the situation worse to stroke my own ego or attempt to get a laugh.

Was that a sign of maturity? Fuck. Was this weird almost-relationship we were in making me an *adult*? I waited for the panic to set in.

5, 4, 3, 2....

Ash was *jealous*. Completely unnecessarily, but that wasn't the point. I didn't want him to be jealous. Didn't want him to feel anything bad, really. What we had going on was supposed to be simple. Fun. Exciting. Not stressful. He was already nervous enough about people finding out about us. I didn't want any other potential dealbreakers to creep in as well.

Wait.

Could there possibly be *even more* problems between us that I had no idea about? Maybe sticking my head in the sand and assuming everything was fine wasn't the way to go after all.

Also, was panicking about Ash's feelings instead of my own a good sign or a bad one?

Why wasn't there a fucking manual on this shit? *What to Do When You Accidently Make Your Best Friend/Bandmate/First Same-Sex Lover Jealous and Maybe Have Other Problems in Your Relationship Too.* There was a catchy title if I'd ever heard one.

Ash stared at me expectantly.

Shit.

With no time to go to the Amberwood Library and search for said manual, I guess I had to figure out how to deal with this myself.

I took a deep breath.

"Jasmine's been a great colleague...," I started carefully. "She's become a friend. I have no idea if she's straight or into men at all. And even if she is, I'm not interested. She's a huge asset to Indigo House and Heartbeat. That's all."

Ash looked at me like he wasn't quite sure if he should believe me.

I scooted closer to him, dipping down slightly and using my head as a crowbar to separate his crossed arms from his chest, forcing him to wrap his arms around me. He grumbled but gave in. Our bodies were touching from top to toes. I kissed his lower lip lightly and snuggled closer.

Ash sighed. "I said I'm *not* jealous," he repeated, with slightly less tension in his voice than before.

I nodded against him solemnly, still not believing his words but choosing to humor him.

Look at me nailing this relationship thing.

We stayed like that for a moment or two. These had quickly become my favorite times with him. I had never been much of a cuddler in the past; hell, more often than not I was out the door as soon as the condom came off. With Ash, I could lie with him for hours and never get squirmy.

Eventually Ash shifted and met my eyes.

"What about you, though?" Ash's voice was shaky as he looked up at me with sincerity. "Aren't you straight?" he asked, continuing on the conversation about Jasmine.

I wasn't sure yet how to instigate a big conversation about us, but at the very least I could be honest about what he was asking. Take the question as a positive first step.

Not sure exactly how to respond, I went for the truth, the best I was able to provide.

"I'm not sure what I am anymore. All I know is this feels right."

Ash

Leeds, United Kingdom

"WHERE the fuck were you last night?" Dean accosted me as soon as I walked into the hotel restaurant for breakfast.

We had half an hour before our bus rolled out, driving us to our next destination. Away from the disaster that had been Leeds.

I grabbed a croissant and stuck it between my teeth as I filled a bowl of cereal. My head hurt. My body ached. I was too damn old for this shit. I didn't drink to excess often anymore, especially when we were in the middle of so many back-to-back shows. This was a clear reminder of why I abided by that principle.

Last night was an exception to all my rules. A string of horrible decisions. A mistake.

"I thought you were gonna come out with me?" Dean continued, his voice loud and abrading my eardrums. "Nobody had any idea where you went. You didn't get on the bus after the show."

"I never said I was going out with you. And I told Cory I was taking off," I said, the sound coming out muffled around the pastry.

Aggressively, I opened two creamers and dumped the contents into my coffee. Picking up the mug and the cereal bowl, I sulked over to a corner booth, away from the table where Dean had settled.

Don't follow me, don't follow me, don't follow me, I pleaded in my mind… to no avail.

Dean dragged a chair from nearby to my booth and positioned it close to me. The metal legs screeched on the tile floor, making me wince.

"What the hell is up with you?" Dean demanded as he took a seat.

The anger and hurt in his voice lost some of their impact as he set down his oversized bowl of Fruity Pebbles. Somehow the colorful cereal annoyed me even more. Could he not be a fucking grown-up for once in his goddamn life?

"I just wanna eat my fucking food and get out of this shittyass town." I slammed my hand down in frustration, almost yelling now. A few other hotel guests looked at me dubiously for disturbing their breakfasts.

Dean dropped his voice, his tone worried. He knew better than anyone this wasn't like me. "Ashy?"

I sighed, scrubbing my face. "I'm fine." I took a calming breath, trying to relax and make this whole town and all my embarrassment disappear. "How was the club?" I asked Dean, my voice back under control, attempting to get Dean talking so I didn't have to. "As good as everyone said?"

He looked at me strangely; thoughts I didn't understand flashed across his eyes.

"I didn't go," he said quietly, pushing the Pebbles around in his bowl. "I tried to track you down all night. Left you like ten messages. Didn't you check your phone?"

Guilt crept into my gut. I opened and shut my mouth a few times, trying to figure out what to say. Had he really spent all night looking for me? Surely Cory would have told him I was doing my own thing, if he'd asked. Not that I gave Cory details, but I made sure our manager knew I was okay. I hadn't thought anyone else would have even noticed I left. Carter spent most nights on video calls with Chase. Something was clearly going on between Beau and Jamie, the dancer who had just joined the tour. Dean was supposed to have gone out.

"I, um, I turned it off," I said.

Dean nodded slowly after a beat, like he wanted to say something else.

"I'm sorry." I winced. My head throbbed with the hangover. "I didn't think you'd care. You had plans."

My gaze became fixated on the white-tiled floor. The grout needed cleaning. I traced along a crack with my shoe.

"I invited you to come," Dean said with a sad smile. "I was worried about you."

Failure hit me square in the chest. I had fucked up. I had let Dean down. Disappointed him. Scared him. He gave up his evening to make sure I was okay. And for what? So I could go to a separate club without him. A *gay* club. So I could try to figure out if these feelings

I'd been having had merit. So I could have a few drinks.
Dance with a guy. Let myself get picked up.

So I could follow the guy into a dirty bathroom.
Touch him. Kiss him. Rake my fingers through his pin-
straight hair, which felt all wrong. Let him pull down
my underwear and drop to his knees, only to panic and
run flying out of the stall as soon as his lips touched
my cock.

To end up alone in my hotel room, sobbing,
with tiny bottles of cheap vodka from the minibar
surrounding me. Embarrassed and alone and utterly
heartbroken.

Knowing for sure that this wasn't a phase or an
experiment. Knowing I was attracted to guys. Knowing
no man would ever measure up to the one I couldn't
have.

"I'm sorry," I said again with an apologetic shrug.

Dean's expression lightened. His tight-lipped
expression evened out. His eyes twinkled. Nothing ever
stayed serious for long with Dean. I had apologized.
We'd get over it. End of story.

"Come on," he said with a wink. "Let's get on the
bus before Cory finds a reason to grump at me."

"You'd probably deserve it," I said with a half
smile.

"So I hear there's this club in Newcastle…," he
started, pushing a still-damp curl from a recent shower
off his forehead. "Just opened a couple months ago—"

"No," I cut him off.

"Come on, Ashy! You totally owe me!"

I rolled my eyes and opened the door for him,
tuning him out as he continued talking. The morning
sunlight made my eyeballs rebel. I silently vowed to
concentrate on the rest of the tour, forgetting about LA

and Leeds and focusing on the music. Dean was my friend, nothing more. When I got home, maybe I would be in a better place to explore things with another guy. A guy who wanted the same things. A guy who made sense. Yes. I would put some distance between Dean and me for a few months after the tour. Live by myself for a bit in my own house. Move on.

Finally.

Ash

AFTER Dean and I had cleared the air, I could breathe so much easier. I had to admit, I had been acting like a jealous jerk around the Indigo House director, when she had been nothing but nice to both of us. Her flirting with Dean was obvious to anyone who paid attention. I should be used to it by now, people flirting with Dean. Groupies did it all the time at meet and greets after Thorns's concerts. It always got on my nerves, but it had never made me crazy the way it had with Jasmine.

I kissed Dean's hand before we stepped out of the car, needing one last point of contact before we kept it platonic for the day. Considering we were going to a LGBTQ+ center, it felt hypocritical to hide what had quickly become one of the best parts of my life; however, I wasn't ready to break out of the safe bubble Dean and I had created.

"Ready for this?" he asked as he pulled his favorite bass out of the trunk.

"Hopefully." I shot him a wink and a broad smile.

We were welcomed into the center by Jasmine and another couple of the staff we'd gotten to know. There was quite a crowd gathered in the lounge area, far more young people than had been there for any of our previous visits. Jasmine told us she wasn't publicly advertising that Dean and I were teaching the sessions as she didn't want to create chaos with our presence—so fucking weird we were famous enough for that to be a possibility—or overshadow the upcoming concert. That being said, all of the regular Indigo House kids were informed this was happening, and clearly there was interest.

Jasmine got everyone's attention and made a short welcome speech. She discussed the upcoming renovations for the music space as a result of the concert fundraiser, described the scope and purpose of Heartbeat, and introduced Dean and me. There was enthusiastic applause when she said our names, which made my face go red. It was funny—I could play in front of a crowd of thousands, yet being commended privately by a small group of underprivileged kids made me duck my head in embarrassment. Thorns's accolades were becoming more impressive each year, but I was still simply regular old Ash.

The three of us had decided that the first session would be super low-key. We would put out all the different instruments we had acquired and see which each of the kids gravitated toward. Dean and I would circulate and give them some basic instruction—or more accurately, I would give them instruction, and Dean would make dumb jokes and generally show support. It was important to Dean that everyone had the opportunity to see what they liked and what they might want to pursue. I agreed that it was a good way to gauge interest levels and was proud of the amount of thought Dean had put into the whole day.

As it turned out, when it was one-on-one, the kids were incredibly shy around Dean and me. Somehow we hadn't accounted for them potentially being starstruck when we were planning the session. Fortunately Dean had the inherent ability to make almost anyone comfortable, and so he fluttered around the room, making friends with everyone and putting any nerves at ease. I instinctively kept seeking him out through the afternoon for looks of reassurance. It was hard to keep my eyes off him anytime these days. Whenever I tracked him down, he was laughing with the kids and the handful of parents, completely in his element. I'd had no idea this was something Dean would have been interested in doing, but he was a natural. Far more so than I was.

Making my way between instrument stations, I checked on everyone and gave a few pointers. At the next session, we would actually begin proper instruction on the instruments. The smiles on the kids' faces when they learned a chord or two were pretty freaking fantastic. Music had literally always been a part of my life. My dad constantly tells the story about how I played "Happy Birthday to You" to myself on the piano when I turned two. It was easy to take that for granted. I was grateful that today reminded me of the simple joy of making a sound, of learning to express oneself through music.

A couple of the kids in particular were already showing lots of enthusiasm and promise. I took the opportunity to draw a few basic music staffs and notes on the whiteboard Jasmine had found for us. As I was teaching the names of the notes in the bass clef, Dean wandered over with his instrument thrown over his shoulder.

"Hey, Dean, will you play us what Ash wrote, on your bass?" Naomi, one of the loudest pupils, requested.

"No can do, sunshine," Dean said.

A chorus of protest rose up from Naomi and the rest of the kids who were paying attention to my impromptu lesson.

"Why not?" Naomi finally demanded.

"Yeah, why not, Dean?" I prompted with a playful smirk.

I knew full well why Dean refused the request. It was something I had been on him about for years, but he was always so freaking stubborn.

Dean scoffed, his cheeks pinking in a way I didn't often see with him. Was he embarrassed?

"Okay, okay, I admit it. I don't know how to read music!" Dean held his hands up in front of himself. He laughed self-deprecatingly. The room quieted down.

"But… how do you learn the songs?" one of the younger kids—I think their name was RJ—asked cautiously.

"Well, mostly we write our own music," Dean responded. "I make up the bass parts myself, or one of the guys will teach me what to do. I'll copy a note they play on the piano or play it by ear. I wish I'd learned when I was younger, but I do okay."

His answer was humble, not bragging about the skill of picking up sounds by ear. Not creating a sob story about exactly how long it sometimes takes him to get a piece right. The other three of us in Thorns were usually pretty patient, knowing it would always take Dean longer than the rest of us to pick up a song.

RJ nodded, looking satisfied with that answer.

"Y'all should learn the proper way, though. Don't do what I did," Dean went on. "Actually, Ashy, here's an idea. Why don't you point to the notes you have there on the board. Everyone can call out what the note is, and then I can play it on the bass? That'll help you guys to learn the notes and maybe you guys can even teach me to read what Ash wrote."

I stared at Dean, a little in awe at the suggestion. He was so effortlessly good with the kids. Dean didn't brood about the past and the fact that his mom couldn't afford music lessons for him. He didn't make up an excuse as to why he had never bothered to learn as an adult, even though I had encouraged him to do so multiple times. He didn't even dwell on the fact that he was convinced he got by fine without reading music and had made it this far without putting in the effort. He simply came up with a positive solution that got the kids on the right path and made them excited to try to "help" him.

Jasmine had paused what she was doing across the room and was also watching Dean's antics with a smile on her face. I fought the urge to scowl or make a big stink about it. Dean had a natural gravitational pull. Jasmine cared about her work and the kids she helped.

Plus it was me who Dean grinned at after he was plugged into the small amp and ready to start.

"Okay, everyone, this note is a…?" I prompted, pointing to a random note on the scale I had drawn.

"B!" the kids cried out in perfect synchronicity.

Dean moved his fingers into position and let the B note sing on his strings.

Dean

RIDING the high of the first session, Ash and I spent the next morning together at his piano, working on the curriculum plan for Heartbeat. We wanted to have a few lessons under our belts before the full project was unveiled publicly at the upcoming concert.

Plus I had a favor I needed to ask him.

"Hey, um, Ashy?" I started, surprisingly nervous.

Ash lifted his hands from the keys and looked at me.

"I was thinking," I said. "After yesterday. Maybe it might be good if I could read music, you know? I'll probably never be very good at it or whatever. But I'd like to try. Could you, um, could you maybe teach me?"

It took a lot of resolve for me to ask. Ash had been on me since high school about reading music. It'd always seemed like a lot of work, and I was already playing the bass well enough that it didn't seem to matter. I'd never felt like it had held me back, but now that I was thinking about it, maybe the band had been making some concessions on the bass lines for me.

Even though I'd made it into a dumb joke, it bothered me that I had to tell the kids I couldn't help them. I wanted Ashy to be proud of me, and I knew that he wouldn't give me too hard a time for finally coming around and asking for help.

Ash gave me a funny look. A dozen emotions passed through his eyes as I waited eagerly for his response. Finally he nodded.

"Sure," he said. "I can teach you."

I breathed a sigh of relief, grateful it was always so simple with him. Yes, we joked and bullshitted a lot, but Ashy knew me so well. He knew by my tone I was being serious, and he didn't give me grief even though he easily could have.

Ash pulled out a couple of sheets of staff paper from his expensive-looking notebook.

"Okay, we'll stick to the bass clef for now as that's basically what you use. Just be aware that most instruments use the treble clef and that has its own set of rules."

I nodded as Ash drew some notes and symbols on the page. I'd been around music for long enough to recognize some of it. Ash explained everything in a slow, easy tone that made it all sound so simple. I was sure it got infinitely more complicated once you got into it.

Note by note, we went up and down the scale on the page. He mirrored the tones on the keyboard and recited the letters. I mentally went through the fingering on my bass guitar, fighting to embed the lesson into my memory.

The process was time-consuming. I had never been a quick learner. But as Ash had been in high school when he spent hours with me in the diner, he was unhurried and went through the lesson over and over until I got it.

He showed me the basics, concepts he had probably understood completely since grade school. Ash made me want to continue learning. He didn't push, and he encouraged me when I was struggling to remember something. I had the passing thought that in another lifetime, Ash would have made a fantastic teacher: history or music or probably any subject of his choosing. He was infinitely patient, mature beyond his years. He loved to learn and was unwaveringly supportive. Kindhearted. Calm.

After an hour I could at least identify the notes I played on a page and understood how to break down the music into bars. I was a long way from being able to actually play Thorns songs at our usual tempo off written music, but it was a first step that I was proud to have taken.

"Thank you, Ashy," I said sincerely when we were finishing up.

Looking at Ash so closely now, his gray eyes so intense, I almost put together the courage to come out with what I really wanted to say to him.

Each day we grew closer. Each day it would hurt more to lose what we were building. Ash and I were so damn good together. I'd never had this sort of connection with anyone. But asking him to go full-in with me wasn't like recruiting his help with Heartbeat, or even like requesting my own music lessons. Everything was on the line here. There would be no turning back from this.

Ash

DEAN and I were so wrapped up in his music lesson, I lost track of time and nearly forgot about our scheduled band meeting. As much as I teased him, Dean asking for music lessons wasn't something I had expected. Maybe it was out of embarrassment for not being able to support the kids, or maybe he finally just decided it was time. Either way, the genuineness in his eyes when he asked me for help made me fall for him even more.

Plus getting to sit that close to him on the piano bench during the lesson was far from a hardship.

Outside of a few casual calls, the Thorns hadn't been together in over two months. The benefit for Indigo House was coming up quickly, and we needed to begin working on our set list. Getting down to business, I rested my laptop on the top of my upright piano so the camera would show both Dean and myself. It wasn't lost on me that after the last time we'd chatted with the guys like this, Dean and I had ended up hooking up for the second time. That wasn't all that long ago, yet somehow it also felt like it had been forever.

"Hey, guys!" I greeted Carter and Beau as the video call connected on my computer.

"How have you two been doing in Amberwood?" Beau asked.

"We've been busy little gophers, haven't we, Ashy?" Dean told the group. He went on to describe Heartbeat and how successful the first day had been. The pride in his voice was evident, even though he was back to full showman mode with the others around.

"Wow, guys, that's so fantastic. I wish we could have been there more to help," Carter said when Dean finally stopped talking.

The four of us chatted for a long time, catching each other up on everything that had been going on over the summer. Chase finally graduated from Juilliard—with honors. He and Carter had been spending time at this cottage they had stayed in last year in the Hamptons. After they had been apart for so long, it was nice that they had some extended time off to be together. Beau and Jamie were in New York. Jamie was teaching at some fancy summer dance intensive, which sounded like it had been going well.

After we were all up to date, we got down to business, planning the set for the concert.

"So I've actually got something I wanted to run by you all," Carter said. "Chase and I have been playing around with a new track we're both super stoked about. It's kind of a fight song, and we think this show would be the perfect debut for it. I know we're still not talking seriously about the next album, but this song could be a single for it when we're ready. If you're all into it, of course."

"Hells yes, we wanna hear it," Dean jumped in enthusiastically.

"Cool. Chase, did you want to play it?" Carter looked off-screen briefly to where his boyfriend must have been sitting.

Chase appeared in Carter's window, and we greeted him. The keyboard must have been just below the camera view as we couldn't see Chase's hands when he began to play. Carter himself was an accomplished pianist, but seeing those two collaborate on the music they wrote together was a special treat.

As the song wound on, I started to get a funny feeling while listening to the lyrics. Like I was missing something or there was a catch of some sort. It was a kickass track, high energy and perfect to dance to. The title—"Stained Glass Cathedrals and Chantilly Lace"—was repeated in the chorus throughout the song. It was an LGBTQ+ anthem, describing how the singer couldn't stand old-timey romance traditions and wanted to form their own. I was completely in love with it by the time the final notes sounded on Chase's keys.

"Wow, guys. That was fantastic. Beyond fantastic," I said.

Chase and Carter grinned at each other with the praise.

"Can totally picture the fans going crazy for it," Dean added, nodding. "You're right that it's the perfect tune for this gig."

"Beau?" Carter prompted the last member of the group to give the song the green light. We were collaborative in all our music. For the most part, we were on the same page, though there had been times in the past when we were divided on whether a song would make the cut. We'd long since agreed all four members of the Thorns needed to approve a song before we put our names on it.

"Yeah, it's brilliant. I love it," Beau said and then paused. A shit-eating smile bloomed on his face. "Interesting lyrics. Anything you guys wanna share with the group?"

Carter's cheeks went bright red a split second before he dropped his head to cover a massive smile. Chase giggled loudly.

Cathedrals, lace. Holy crap. Were they going to tell us…?

"We're engaged!" Chase blurted out, holding up his left hand, which now sported a platinum ring.

The call erupted in excitement as we all started talking over each other. Congratulations to the happy couple were offered freely, and Dean started screeching out an off-key version of the wedding march.

"That's amazing, guys. I'm stupidly happy for you," I said.

"Do we get to hear the story of how it happened?" Beau asked.

"Not that excit—" Carter started.

"It was perfect," Chase said at the same time. He looked at his boyfriend—*fiancé*—and pouted at Carter's words.

"You go," Carter conceded, laughing.

Those two were too freaking sweet together.

"Like I was *saying*"—Chase grinned at Carter—"it was perfect. He took me outside to this field of wildflowers and set up this beautiful picnic. When I opened the picnic basket, there was a bouquet of lavender inside—lavender flowers have been a thing for us since we were kids—and the bouquet had a ring around the stems. Carter was on one knee when I turned around. So romantic."

Chase kissed Carter's cheek while the rest of us fawned over their story. I couldn't say I was a particularly sentimental guy; I'd never thought much about weddings or any of that before. But Chase was so joyful he deserved to have everyone gush over his big moment. They'd gone through a lot to be together, and I couldn't be happier for them. Our childhood friend was growing up.

Dean

"THAT'S exciting—Chase and Carter," I said to Ash once we had wrapped up the band meeting.

"Yeah, I'm so happy for them. It's great news," Ash replied, shutting the lid of his laptop and putting it safely into a carrying case.

After closing the cover over the piano keys, I shifted out from behind the instrument and tucked in the bench. Turning to Ash I put my hands on my hips, ready to confront the very serious issue now at hand.

"If you get best man over me I'm gonna be so pissed at you."

Ash rolled his eyes, seemingly unbothered by our friendship-changing predicament. Unbelievable.

"I'm sure he'll ask Beau," Ash replied calmly.

Dammit. I forgot about Beau.

I considered my options and recovered quickly. "Maybe I should start a campaign. I'll need a catchy slogan. Something that rhymes. Or possibly an alliteration."

I pursed my lips, thinking about the perfect word to combine with my name that would convince Carter to pick me.

"Something like… 'Beau for Best Man'?" Ash suggested uncooperatively.

Wow, he was being unhelpful. The fact that Beau's name *happened* to begin with the same letter as "best man" certainly didn't help my case. But Ash didn't need to point that out quite so sensibly.

I stuck my tongue out at him.

"Beau would plan, like, the lamest bachelor party ever." I pouted. "I'd be way better than Beau."

"What about… 'Drama Queen Dean'?" Ash taunted me with a smirk. "That's got an alteration *and* a rhyme!"

He bopped my nose as I stared at him in confounded insult.

"Drama queen's not even a wedding position." I sulked, crossing my arms like a petulant child.

"Clearly you don't go to many weddings. There's *always* a drama queen." Ash put his arms around me and playfully nipped my neck, softening his tone. "Carter's going to ask you to be in the wedding party without you needing to campaign."

I sighed, resigning myself to a lower position on the wedding hierarchy. Stupid Beau. And stupid Ash's stupid logic.

"I still can't believe they're engaged," Ash continued. "It seems like just esterday Carter was giving that speech about Chase at the *Grammys*."

"I know," I said with a half smile at the memory. "Do you remember how freaked out he was when he came off the stage after he said all that? I thought he was gonna use the Grammy as a puke bucket."

"Gross!" Ash exclaimed, wrinkling his nose.

"Can't say I blame him, though. It was such a ballsy move." I stepped closer to Ash, looking up at him through my lashes. "He had no idea what Chase's deal was. If he wanted Carter back. Where his head was at."

"Uh-huh," Ash said quietly, drawing his arms tighter around me.

The room was quiet except for the sound of our breathing. We hadn't turned on the lights before our call—relying on the ambiance from the windows—but the clouds had come in, and the room had grown dark. It was like we were the only people in the world. Like everything that existed was in that room. The two of us. Our bodies growing closer. Our heartbeats getting faster. Falling in sync. My words were about Chase and Carter, but Ash knew I was talking about us.

"He was just trusting what they had," I went on. "Trusting their friendship. Knowing if he didn't do something, he might always regret it."

I recognized things would change soon when the rest of the band got here in person in a few days. The bubble Ash and I had built over the past two months had a time limit. It always had; it was simply more palpable now that it was coming to an end. Ash seemed to be growing more comfortable with the idea of us; however, it was obvious he still had hesitations.

But I knew what I wanted. There was one line that we hadn't crossed yet.

"Come upstairs with me, Ashy," I whispered.

Ash

DEAN led me into my bedroom, which had become *our* bedroom for the past month. All of his things were in here, and we hadn't spent a night apart in weeks. I had grown acquainted with his body in this room. Studied his moans, his sighs. Learned how much I could ache for someone's touch. We had done almost everything two people could do together in this room. And I had savored every minute of it.

"I want you inside me," Dean whispered between kisses.

His words were soft, but they rang out clearly in the silence. They made my breath catch in my throat. My stomach lurched. I pulled back enough to be able to look into his eyes.

"A-are you sure?" I asked.

He nodded, a combination of vulnerability and trust radiating from his gaze. Brushing the perfect ringlet curl from his forehead, I kissed the spot unveiled. I kissed his temple, across his cheekbone, down his nose. He stood on his toes to meet my lips, taking what he wanted from me confidently.

It was easy like this. In the quiet. In the dark. All that mattered here was him and me. Bodies. Heartbeats. We were on even ground in the dark. I could pretend for a while that he wanted me in all the same ways I wanted him.

Desperate to touch the miles of his silky skin, I stripped off Dean's shirt. I traced the powerful muscles in his back, long since mapped and memorized, with my fingers. I licked down the corded tendons of his throat, finding the spot behind his ear that made him crazy. Dean gasped against me, struggling with shaky hands to rid me of my shirt. I loved that I had that effect on him with something so simple. His body was putty in my hands, and bringing him pleasure was like nothing else on earth.

Dean undid his pants and shimmied the tight fabric down over his hips. As always, the lack of underwear was ridiculously sexy. I'm sure it couldn't possibly have been comfortable—especially when his cock was as hard as it was now—but *damn*. I followed his lead, shucking my jeans and boxers until we were bare against each other.

He pulled me closer to my bed. Or was it me who pushed him? It was so mutual, the need. We tumbled together to the soft mattress, clutching at each other for purchase. His body looked small under mine as I trapped him between my arms, yet he was anything but weak. Dean pulled my hips down flush to his. We both groaned at the contact, and he immediately rolled against me, seeking friction.

My lips caught his in a ravaging kiss. I sucked his tongue into my mouth, stroking it with my own. Desire and hunger and lust mashed together. I couldn't think. Could only feel. I was so caught up in his body, it didn't even occur to me to consider the magnitude of what we were doing. The line we were crossing. How difficult it would be to go back from this.

Dean reached over to what had become his nightstand. He pulled out the bottle of lube I had grown *really* fond of over the past few months, and a condom. Staring at the foil packet, a sudden fear hit me.

"Do you, um, have any idea what to do here?" I asked, my cheeks heating in embarrassment.

Sure, I'd watched a shit-ton of gay porn over the past few months, but that didn't ever show the important stuff. The lead-up. The prep. Why the fuck hadn't I thought to do any research before now?

Because you've been terrified to admit how much you want this, my brain supplied unhelpfully. I ignored my self-deprecating thoughts in favor of everything else going on.

"On my end of things or on yours?" Dean asked with a smirk. He ran his fingers up and down my chest, playing with the smattering of hair absently.

The thought of him with anyone else made me recoil. "Actually, on second thought, I don't wanna know."

I fought the urge to turn away from him in mortification at the conversation. Terrified of my own naïveté. Of how desperate I was to take this step with him. Fought away the images of my awkward younger self when I lost my virginity with a woman. Dean was so naturally confident; this whole situation made it clear how uneven our foundation was. This was easy for him, not a big deal. It meant *everything* to me.

"Hey," Dean said softly. He put his hand on my cheek and forced me to face him. I looked into his eyes—the sincerity and the caring—and I relaxed. He kissed me gently. "I've never done this either. Either side. I just trust you."

His words melted me. The tension and unease I had been harboring—the thoughts of not measuring up—had been instantly erased. I kissed him harder again. Our noses knocked together as I tried to bury my tongue in Dean's throat. My cock had deflated a little through our awkward conversation, but it went rigid again against his hip. He grasped at my back as I moved on top of him. I spread his legs with my thigh. Dean's admission hung in the air. In his breathless gasps. In his fingers as they clawed at my spine. We moved as one, struggling to get closer. Needing each other in a carnal way I had never imagined before.

We figured it out together. I stretched him slowly with my fingers until he was thrusting back against me. Watching his masculine body yield to mine was the sexiest thing I had seen in my life. I was terrified when I finally began to enter him. He was so small and my cock was… not. I was scared to cause him pain, scared he would need me to stop. Scared I would come in five seconds flat. Scared that my heart would shatter with the intensity of it all.

But regardless of what was happening to his body, Dean was still Dean.

"Fucking come on, Ash. I learned to play the bass faster than this."

"No you didn't," I said through gritted teeth. "And shut up, I'm concentrating."

"Shut up?" Dean raised his eyebrows in mockery. "Exactly what every dude dreams of hearing his boyfr—*guy* say at a time like this."

I ignored his innocent slip of the tongue with the label I really didn't need to think about right now.

No matter how giddy it secretly made me.

Instead, I forced myself to focus on the task in front of me. I inched into him and watched his face for any sign of discomfort. Regardless of his bantering words, his goading wasn't going to make me risk hurting him.

Dean cupped my jaw and ran his thumb along my cheekbone.

"Why don't we try this?" he said gently.

He shifted until the fraction of my dick I had been able to get inside him slipped out. Dean rolled me onto my back. He nipped the lobe of my ear playfully before whispering, "You're not going to hurt me" directly into my ear.

The heat of his mouth, combined with the sweet words, erased any thoughts of failure that had been looming over my head.

Then he straddled my hips.

Dean moved above me, holding my cock steady and guiding himself closer. While he was still moving slowly, he was far less cautious than I had been. When I slipped through the first ring of muscle, I fought the urge to shove in farther as fast as possible. Fuck. It was so, *so* good.

He settled his weight on me, and every muscle in my body throbbed with adrenaline. Dean began to swivel his hips, growing more experimental with his movements with each passing second. I let him do what felt good for him; his tight heat and his broken gasps brought me more than my fair share of pleasure.

I reached to stroke his neglected cock, surprised to find it completely hard and straining toward his belly.

"Oh God," he cried when I wrapped my hand around him.

Sex hadn't been anywhere near this good before. I'd never been this attracted to a woman. Never felt the same jittery excitement, the tingly happiness, the butterflies. Never experienced the bone-crushing jealousy. Nothing had ever made sense in the same way before.

Staying hard was certainly not a problem now.

He rode me faster. His powerful thighs strained around my hips as I slid in and out of his body. Dean's masculine form hovered above me—his broad shoulders, his tapered waist. His chest glistened with sweat. His cock leaked into my hand. Those perfect curls bounced in a way that was unfairly erotic. He arched his back; I hit a new angle inside him that caused him to cry out.

I was struck with the same thought as during our first fumbling encounter together: this was how it was *supposed* to be.

My hips snapped up to meet Dean's. I rubbed him faster. It was too good to last much longer. I threw my head back against the pillow. Sounds I had no idea I was capable of tumbled out of my throat. I snaked my other hand between his legs and caressed the delicate skin beside his entrance with my thumb. God it was sexy that his body stretched like that to accommodate mine.

Stroking Dean's cock in double time, I was desperate for him to fall apart while I was still inside him.

"Come for me, baby," I said.

The pet name was unscripted and certainly implied more than the sex-only relationship we had established up until now. Dean's eyes flew open at the word, and I felt the glorious tensing of all his muscles a beat later. His ass clenched hard around my cock, squeezing me impossibly tighter inside his body. I looked down at my chest covered in Dean's pearly release, gasping at how sexy it was. The room seemed to shake as pleasure flooded my veins. My orgasm came screaming out of me, a blistering heat that was both overwhelmingly intense and utterly uncontrollable. I filled the condom with shot after shot. Fuck, I wished the latex barrier wasn't separating us.

My pleasure seemed to last forever, but once I regained awareness of my surroundings, my gaze floated to the man above me. His too-long ringlet curls were in his eyes… again. The look of complete bliss on his face melted me.

Dean was the most ridiculous, irresponsible, likely straight, *frustrating* man I'd ever met. And now, somehow, I'd fallen completely in love with him.

Ash

"PERFECT, that's right! Doesn't it feel more natural to hold the bow that way?" I asked RJ, one of the kids we were working with at Indigo House.

We were well into the lessons, and attendance had been crazy. A lot of the students had been showing up at every session. Some—like RJ—had been making a lot of progress. Others hadn't been catching on as quickly, but honestly I wasn't convinced that was the point. The confidence I had seen growing from within these kids, the pride in learning something new, the self-expression from creating music, the budding bonds between them all—those were far and away the takeaways Dean and I hoped to inspire.

RJ nodded at the correction, testing out the new grip on the cello bow. They ran the bow across the D string. It was still kind of a screechy mess, but there was definite improvement over the first lesson. After giving RJ a couple more pointers and some scales to work on, I took a step back to see what else I could offer as suggestions or encouragement.

A short guy wearing painted-on jeans and a dress shirt with one too many buttons undone came up next to me.

"RJ's really loving the class," he said, extending his hand for me to shake. "I'm Jax, RJ's brother."

"Ash. Nice to meet you," I replied.

"As if you need to introduce yourself." Jax laughed, a high-pitched sound that I could already tell would get annoying quickly.

His eyes drifted up and down my body in a way that made me more than a little uncomfortable. I awkwardly tried not to notice.

"Um," I said, unsure how to respond.

I was somewhat used to people knowing who I was with the success of the band, but what was I supposed to do? Not introduce myself when I met someone? That seemed rude and way too cocky. It was far more usual for folks not to know who I was than for them to recognize me. Things were different for Carter and Dean and sometimes even for Beau. However, I was the unobtrusive guy hidden behind a drum kit most of the time.

Jax jumped in again before I had to think of something to say. "RJ talks about you constantly. I was starting to think you were too good to be true."

I forced a smile, not wanting to be impolite. "RJ's a great kid. It's been good getting them out here regularly. Got a lot of raw talent in this group."

Looking across the room covertly, I was hoping someone would need my assistance. Unfortunately all the kids looked to be busy and engaged in what they were doing for the moment.

"Is there anything we should be doing at home? To help RJ practice?" Jax asked.

"From my experience a lot has to come from them. Motivation is the most important factor. Encourage, don't push. Show that you're interested."

Jax nodded, absorbing my words. This was easier; I could talk about music for hours.

"There are a lot of resources online too," I added. "If you're interested I can write down a couple of sites for you to check out."

"Yeah, that would be great."

"Sure. I've gotta check on some of the other kids, but remind me before you leave if I forget."

I made my way across the room, checking on the group. Jax seemed genuinely supportive of his younger sibling. All of the kids here deserved support. I focused on that instead of the uncomfortable vibe Jax had given me. Besides that one time in the gay club in Leeds, I'd never blatantly been hit on by a guy before. Or maybe I had, but I just hadn't realized it at the time. I could be pretty clueless about that kind of stuff. Always had been. I brushed it off. Jax's flirting hadn't meant anything, and I had enough complicated shit going on right now. Nobody came close to measuring up to the guy on the other side of the room.

The guy who was currently laughing with Jasmine. Standing slightly too close for my liking. Her dog came flying through the door at that moment and ran directly for Dean. I smiled to myself as Dean dropped to his knees, giving Bella his full attention. He was so damn cute with that dog. With any animal, really.

As sweet as the scene was, it also paralyzed me. It was these small, benign moments where Dean *was just Dean*—moments that most people wouldn't blink twice at—that terrified me the most. I seemed to notice these with increased frequency recently. Moments where he would magically turn a Heartbeat kid's frustration into joyous laughter with a well-timed joke. Moments where he would read a story to Gracie at nap time and fully commit to making all the barnyard animal sounds in the book. Moments where—even though he barely had two minutes to himself these days—he would help lonely Mrs. Hannagan across the street with her groceries and then accept her invitation to join her for tea.

Mundane moments that reminded me exactly who Dean was. Without the bravado. The groupies. The fame.

The same person he had been since elementary school.

The person I had been falling in love with for fifteen years.

Being with Dean the other night changed something in me. It wasn't just the sex. Nor was it the feel of his skin on mine. It wasn't the sweat, or the pleasure, or even the mind-numbing kisses.

It was the closeness. The laughter. The feeling of being completely at one with him.

Completely in sync.

More than ever, knowing that feeling had a timeline—an expiry date—made me nauseous. I had no idea how I could go back to being bandmates, let alone best friends, with Dean after experiencing the enormity of our intimacy that night.

But this was temporary. It was *all* temporary.

At some point I would have to find a way to deal with him deciding it was time to move on.

Dean had told me he wasn't interested in Jasmine. I wanted to trust him on that, but she made a hell of a lot more sense for him than I did. If—*when*—he wanted to be with a woman, there was very little I could do about it. Inevitably we would come upon the thorns.

I sighed, fighting the constant sense of inadequacy that bubbled in my chest, and corrected the posture of one of my little piano players.

Dean

"WE'RE all gonna miss you guys after your last session." Jasmine walked up to where I was standing, watching over the room.

Well, mainly watching Ash. And the slutty little twink who was all fucking over him. The older brother of one of our kids. Who was dressed like he was going to a nightclub. This was supposed to be a place of education. Not a hookup joint where he could flirt with *my* boyfriend.

Boyfriend. Was that what Ash was to me? I'd accidently almost called him that the other night. Mercifully I didn't think he'd noticed. And even if he had caught my blunder, he'd had his dick in my ass at the time. I was distracted. Sue me.

The more Ash and I got into this, the harder it was to talk about. I didn't want to rock the boat. Didn't want to give him a reason to pull back from what we were doing. But it was really fucking good between us. I wanted to scream it from the rooftops. Post photos of us together on social media. Scratch that fucking twink's eyes out for having the balls to hit on what was mine.

I wanted my mom to know. Wanted Carter and Beau and Chase and Jamie to know. Wanted to share the most important thing in my world with the people I loved.

I even wanted Cory to know, for Christ's sake! And I *fucking* hated Cory.

No, I didn't hate him.

I sighed.

Why did this have to be so difficult?

"You'll be fine," I told Jasmine, fighting to focus on something other than Ash for a few minutes. "The kids are doing so well. They need a teacher who can be here all the time. But we'll come visit when we can. Don't want Bella-boo to forget about me."

I winked at her, and she laughed. God I loved her doggo.

Ash finally moved away from his admirer. I watched him walk toward the next kid as the twink stared at Ash's ass with no subtlety at all. The momentary relief when Ash ended the conversation was replaced by a foreign, growly sensation in my chest. Since when did I get jealous?

"You've got nothing to worry about," Jasmine said.

I froze at her words, completely silenced. Oh fuck. Had I made my distrust of the stupid, poorly dressed twink that obvious? Wait, had Jasmine caught on to what was going on between Ash and me *before this*?

Oh shit, oh shit, oh shit.

My mind raced and my heart threatened to pump out of my chest. I thought Ash and I had been so careful around her. Around everyone. This was probably my fault. I was terrible at keeping secrets. Ash was going to be so mad at me.

"We're not…," I stammered, unsure what to say. The flat-out denial felt heavy on my tongue.

Jasmine raised her brow. Christ, I was such a horrible liar.

"You stare at each other with the same dopey smile. You're obsessed with each other."

"It's… complicated," I said, unsure about what Ash would want me to do here. Desperately wishing I could mind-control him to walk over and help me deal with this situation.

"She's going to miss you so much. You *better* come visit." Jasmine laughed at me.

The record inside my brain scratched. Wait, what? She? Visit?

At that moment, Bella burst in from playing with some of the kids in the other room, running right toward me. I knelt down to give her head scratches.

"See? Matching dopey smiles," Jasmine said, shaking her head.

Fuck, fuck, fuck.

I replayed what we'd said. "Don't want Bella-boo to forget about me." Jasmine was continuing our banter about her fucking dog. She hadn't somehow caught on about Ash and me because of an across-the-room look or a misplaced grumble. I was so obsessed over Ash I hadn't been paying attention to our conversation. I had been so paranoid about getting caught I had almost spilled the beans myself.

I buried my scorching face in Bella's soft fur, trying to convince a hole in the ground to open up and suck me inside.

Dean

ON Sunday I went to my mom's house for brunch as usual. Ash had an obligation with his own family, so it was just me, my mom, my sisters, Harlow and Maci, and my niece Gracie, in attendance.

It was the first time Ash and I had been apart in a few days. Driving down the familiar roads alone, I turned off the radio and took the opportunity to reflect.

I thought about the upcoming concert. It would be the first time the Thorns had been onstage together for a while. I was ecstatic to see the guys again in a few days. To hear all about Carter and Chase's upcoming nuptials. To cement my rightful position in their wedding party. To see Beau and Jamie and catch up on all they'd been doing all summer. I was looking forward to being back performing for an audience. I thrived in front of a crowd, and I missed the rush of hundreds of fans chanting our lyrics when we played.

I thought about the sex Ash and I'd had the other night. Had that really happened? I'd been thinking about being with Ash like that for a while now, but the real deal was nothing like I had expected. As much as I'd tried to settle Ash's nerves with my own confidence, I'd been *terrified*. Terrified that it would be uncomfortable. Maybe even painful. Or worst of all, that it wouldn't turn me on and I'd somehow let my best friend down. That the fragile tower we'd built would collapse through no fault of our own.

Fortunately all of those fears had turned out to be completely unfounded. It was really fucking good once we'd gotten into it. Ash's gaze on me while I'd ridden him had been the sexiest thing I had seen in a long time. I couldn't say I would want to bottom every day, but maybe Ashy would be willing to trade off or something? I'd have to check in with him to see if that was something he would want to explore.

I thought about my mistake with Jasmine at Indigo House. Christ, this secret was eating me up inside. I was jumpy and paranoid. I was going crazy all the time. It wasn't like me to keep things hidden. My life was usually an open book. For Ash I would do anything it took to keep up what we were doing. But maybe I could convince him to let us come clean to a few people to help decrease the pressure? I wasn't exactly sure why he was so adamant we had to keep all this under wraps, but I would be patient and give him as much time as he needed. He was worth it.

Pulling into my mom's driveway, I looked forward to seeing my crazy family and focused on being in the moment.

The table was decked out already when I arrived. Three vases of fancy-looking flowers lined the center, and the place settings had the cloth napkins my mom always insisted on for brunch. Bowls of summer fruits were scattered about, and the smell of waffles permeated the air. My stomach grumbled in response.

Once all the hellos had been exchanged and Gracie was set up in her high chair, we sat for the feast. I piled my plate sky-high with waffles, strawberries, and squirty whipped cream.

"Beans, how's the music program been going?" Mom asked.

"Eally goo," I mumbled around the massive bite I had shoved in my mouth.

"Watch your damn manners," she scolded me, eyebrow raised in a challenge.

"Sorry." I finished chewing the bite of buttery goodness. "Really good. There's been a great turnout, and the kids love learning from Ash. He's so patient with them."

"What's this for again?" Maci asked. She was a flight attendant, and her schedule sometimes kept her away for a few weeks at a time. Everything with Heartbeat had happened so quickly, I couldn't remember what I'd told her the last time we talked.

"The band got asked to play a charity gig next week. It's to help this struggling community center."

"Oh yeah, you told me about that. The LGBTQ one in Boston, right?" Maci asked.

I took a sip of my fresh-squeezed orange juice. "Yeah. Concert's sold out now, so they should get the fancy new renovation they're planning. Resale value of the tickets is crazy too."

"You got us tickets, right, bestest brother?" she asked.

"I only got two. Gave them to Mom, and she can decide which of you two freeloaders gets the other one."

"Oh, no pressure there…." Mom rolled her eyes.

"Anyway," I continued, "I figured I had some time these days, so Ash and I started a music program for some of the kids they work with."

"My baby brother has a soul after all!" Harlow dramatized, clutching her chest like a silent-film heroine.

Gracie giggled at her mom's theatrics before going back to mashing her blueberries around her tray.

"Hey, I give back!" I argued.

Harlow made a face. "To the groupies, maybe."

Maci burst out laughing. My two sisters began a conversation about some of my exploits over the years—the PG version, thankfully, as there was a baby in the room.

"La, la, la, la," Mom started singing, covering her ears. As if she had ever shied away from the topic of my sex life. Woman was the one who bought me an economy-sized box of condoms as a going-away present for Thorns's first tour.

Gracie covered her ears and started yelling, mimicking Mom. And effectively smushing blueberries into her short blond hair.

"Christ," I muttered under my breath.

Grabbing one of the wet wipes that always seemed to be miraculously close to babies, I reached over to my shrieking niece to clean her hands.

God, this house could be such a disaster sometimes. I wanted to scream over the noise. Yell out my frustrations and shut them all up.

I've been seeing a guy!

That would certainly be one way to do it, wouldn't it? I smiled to myself at the thought as I scrubbed Gracie's blue fingers. Lord knows I loved me some drama, and dropping that bomb when they least expected it would absolutely cause a spectacle.

I thought about my conversation at the petting zoo with Harlow when she told me she was seeing Smelly Feldman—fine, *James* Feldman. She was trying to convince me to settle down like she had finally done. Harlow didn't believe I was capable of monogamy for a second. My family would likely be more shocked that I was serious about someone than at the person's gender.

Practically speaking, I wouldn't necessarily need to tell them it was Ash I had been seeing. Maybe if I told them part of the story, this secret wouldn't weigh me down so much? They would be surprised that I was with a guy, but none of them had a hateful bone in their bodies.

On second thought, there was no way I could do that. Harlow and Maci would unquestioningly beg me to tell them who the guy was. And my mom. Mom would know it was Ash without me saying anything.

Of course it would be Ash.

I sighed. No, I couldn't tell them any of it without giving the whole thing away.

Harlow started talking about day care or some other shit I didn't care about. The collective attention span in my family was all of two minutes.

I kept my lips sealed.

The moment passed.

Dean

"**SO** I almost told my family yesterday," I said to Ash casually the next evening.

We were eating dinner together on his back deck, like we did so often these days. The rest of the band was arriving tomorrow for the concert. Carter, Chase, Beau, and Jamie were all staying with us in Ash's house, meaning I would have to go back to sleeping in a separate room, and Ash and I would have to be strictly platonic around each other. I was more than ready for the guys to know about us, but I knew Ash wasn't.

"You what?" Ash's jaw dropped as he turned to face me. "Jesus, we were together all last night and you're only mentioning this now?"

I chuckled as I traced his forearm with my index finger.

"You came home all hot and sweaty from building your parents' new deck. I had other priorities." I shrugged and waggled my eyebrows at him.

Last night had been *fuuuuun*.

"Be serious for, like, two seconds here," Ash scolded me, covering my roving fingers with his other hand to stall my movement.

"Oh, I am being serious. I think I prioritized you real good. Twice, if I recall."

Ash rolled his eyes. "I don't know why I even *try* to have a serious conversation with you. It's pointless."

"Okay, okay," I said. I took both of his hands in mine and kissed his knuckles in apology. "I'm sorry. I didn't mean to make light of it. I *almost* told them. It's getting harder not to say anything. I'm not used to having secrets."

Ash let out a defeated sigh.

"I know. Me neither. I'm just not ready for other people to know. You haven't told anybody else, right? We haven't really talked about it."

I grimaced. The small gesture slipped out unconsciously before I could hide it. We were sitting so close, Ash noticed it immediately.

"Dean?" he said with a harder edge, challenging me to correct him.

God, I didn't want to cause a fight right now. Things were going so good between us, and I knew the truth was going to piss him off. I was a horrible actor, and lying to Ash wasn't an option I would even consider. Plus it was too much of a risk for him to not know the truth from me directly. Jamie had promised not to say anything, but I couldn't let him walk into our house tomorrow without Ash being aware of the situation. As much as it sucked, I needed to come clean.

Also when did I start thinking of Ash's place as *our* house? I liked that. Maybe too much.

"I may have told Jam-Jam," I admitted.

"Jamie! You told *Jamie*?"

Ash sprang up from his chair. He ran his hands through his hair as he paced back and forth.

"Goddammit, Dean. Why the hell would you tell Jamie!" Ash's voice was shaky. Panicked.

Shit. I knew this was going to be bad.

"I needed to tell someone. I'm sorry, Ashy. It was before anything happened with us. He won't say anything. He promised."

"He's dating our fucking bandmate, Dean! The whole fucking band is gonna know!"

"He won't tell Beau. He wouldn't do that to me. To us." I paused, searching for the right words. I knew this wasn't good, but I needed Ash to understand. "I had all these feelings for you, Ashy. I thought I was going crazy."

Ash scrubbed his hands over his face. I pulled him in to me, wrapping my arms around him from my seated position.

"I never told him anything actually ended up happening between us. For all he knows, it was just a crush."

"And is it?" Ash asked, his tone quieter but still on edge. "A crush? Because I don't know what the fuck is going on here, Dean. One day everything was normal, and the next you came banging on my front door and both our lives got a lot more complicated."

"No." I shook my head. "It's not just a crush, Ashy."

I looked up at him, sensing this was possibly the most important conversation we would ever have. A conversation we'd needed to have for a while. The fragile balance of what we had created had the ability to come toppling down right now with one misinterpreted word. I wanted to tell him that it was so much more than a crush. So much more than sex. That he'd come to mean everything to me, and I wanted to try—*really try*—to have an actual relationship with him. I took a deep breath and continued.

"I want—"

Diiiiing-dooong.

I paused, wrinkling my nose in confusion. Ash lifted his gaze over my shoulder to the front door.

He was clearly pissed at me, but at least he was hearing me out. I really didn't want to answer the door—for whatever politician or kid selling chocolate bars or Mormon missionary who was on the other side to distract us from what I had to say to him.

Diiiiing-dooong.

Christ. Didn't anyone have any patience these days?

"Should we…?" I gestured toward the entryway.

Ash nodded, his eyebrows pulled together in a frown. He moved around the chair I was sitting in, slid the screen door open, and walked into the house. I followed in a daze, not knowing what else to do. This conversation might have been temporarily interrupted, but we needed to continue it. Preferably tonight. Before the band arrived in the morning and we couldn't—

"Surprise!" Carter's voice rang out a split second after Ash opened the front door. "We came early!"

Ash

FUCK.

Fuck.

Fuck, fuck, fuck, fuck, fuck!

It wasn't that I didn't want to see the rest of the guys. But could they seriously not have waited the extra eighteen hours like we'd planned?

I glanced behind me at Dean, whose mouth was open, disbelief written clearly on his face. A fresh wave of panic washed over me. Dean was terrible at hiding anything. How in the bloody hell were we going to keep this secret living in the same house for the next week? Especially before we had really had a chance to talk about it?

"H-hey guys," I said, moving out of the way so they could step into the foyer.

Carter wrapped his arms around me as Chase bounced up and down in excitement beside him. After I welcomed the grooms-to-be, I hugged Beau; I couldn't help but tense when I saw Jamie. I had only known him for a few months, and our interactions had been limited. Now I was suddenly forced to trust him with the biggest secret I'd ever had.

I had a hard time articulating exactly why it was so pivotal that nobody found out about Dean and me. My family and friends were wonderful and I had no doubt that they would be fully accepting if and when I came out to them. Now that I had figured out how I identified, it was even easier to want to share that part of my life with them.

The problem was Dean.

I had stopped questioning his physical attraction to me a few weeks ago, and our sexual chemistry was off the charts. But Dean's attention span was short. His reputation with groupies was well known by every gossip rag out there. Even though our fling had been going on for longer than I'd ever seen him pursue one person, it was indisputably just convenient sex for him. I was here. He was here. Bada bing, bada boom, bada banging.

It was not that for me.

At some point Dean would get bored and that would be that. I had known since the beginning this was only going to end one way: with me getting my heart broken. And that's why I was terrified of involving anyone else in this mess.

When this ended, I didn't want the sympathy, didn't want the awkward stares or the polite encouragement. I didn't want the band to be impacted or, God forbid, the media to find out. No, when this ended I wanted to be able to silently fall apart in private. Mourning the best thing I'd ever had, knowing I would never have it again.

So I put on a brave face, determined to be the best damn hostess since Donna Reed.

I showed both of the couples up to their rooms. As I walked down the hall, I covertly closed the door to the bedroom Dean had supposedly been staying in so nobody could see it was completely empty of luggage or his personal items. He would need to sleep in there for the next week. Maybe he would want to be in there permanently after all this. I hated that we hadn't had one last night together first.

Once everyone was settled, I flicked on the café lights on the beams of the patio and grabbed a couple of the six-packs I had chilling in the fridge. My energy level was low, but I plastered on a smile. We all congregated outside as we caught up on each other's lives. I purposely sat as far apart from Dean as possible, not wanting to automatically touch him and give ourselves away before this little charade even really began. We had been doing a good job of that around Indigo House, but my home had been our safe space. Where we could fully be ourselves.

"So how are the music classes going?" Beau asked.

"Really well," I said.

"Fucking amazeballs!" Dean exclaimed at the same time.

I snorted at Dean's enthusiasm.

"There's this kid RJ. Ashy's teaching them cello. Been, like, a couple fucking lessons, and they can play the whole beginner workbook. And this girl Naomi's learning the guitar? I swear she's gonna be the next Joan Jett with how hard she rocks."

My heart fluttered for Dean's passion for the program. I was more skeptical about any of these kids earning a place in the Rock and Roll Hall of Fame, but who knows? I'd been wrong before. Dean had become a champion for our little group, and seeing him work with and support them all was something special.

"That's so cool you guys are doing that," Carter said, taking a sip of his beer. "Do you think you'll keep going after the concert?"

"Not as regularly, but we want to still be involved," I said. Dean nodded his agreement. "Jasmine, the director of Indigo House, found this awesome teacher to take over permanently. Actually, my mom got some of her symphony friends involved, and she helped with that. Guess it depends on what happens next with the band, but we still want to come back when we're in town."

"Should we start talking about that? What happens next? Another album?" Beau asked.

"I mean, we've already got a new kickass single," Dean said.

"Carter and I have a couple other songs we're working on too," Chase chimed in. "Nothing else is ready to show you yet, but I guess you could say we've been inspired lately." He winked at his fiancé.

"Veto!" Dean said loudly. The rest of the group looked at him with amusement at the outburst. "We've got room for one sappy love song per album. Maximum."

I stared into my glass, avoiding looking at him. Dean's comment was likely intended to be a joke, but it still hit hard. It was clearer than ever where he stood on romance.

"Not love songs necessarily. That wouldn't fit the band," Chase said. He cleared his throat awkwardly. "More, you know, the other thing...." His face turned the color of a strawberry.

"Huh?" Dean blinked rapidly, gears turning in his head while the rest of us figured out what Chase meant.

"Sex, Deano. He means sex," Jamie said helpfully.

We all burst out laughing. I wasn't sure it was possible, but Chase seemed to get even redder.

"Oh fuck yeah. I'm down for that, then." Dean pumped his fist.

The night continued with joking and laughter. I was quiet, but I was usually the quietest member of the group when we were all together, so nobody called me on it. It was good to see them all again, a night for us to hang out and be together before we started rehearsing for the concert. Even if it wasn't the evening I had planned for myself and Dean, it turned out to be a pretty good time in the end.

Dean

AFTER the other four guys had turned in for the night, I rapped my knuckles as quietly as I could against Ashy's closed bedroom door. My toothbrush, along with everything else I owned, was still in Ash's room after the unexpected interruption.

Ash answered the door, wearing only a pair of low-slung pajama bottoms. It was more than he usually wore to bed when we were together, but somehow his having something on was even sexier than seeing him completely naked. He held his finger to his mouth to keep me quiet before pulling back the door so I could sneak inside. After he closed the door behind me silently, we turned to face each other.

Unable to resist any longer, I reached for his hips and stepped into his space to kiss him. His skin was warm beneath my palms.

So much had been left unsaid between us when the band barged in. It was horrible timing, right when we were on the verge of being completely honest with each other.

Ash pushed at my chest reluctantly.

"We can't," he whispered. "This has to stop, Dean."

"I know." I nodded, my head heavy on my shoulders. "I just needed to do that once more."

It wasn't the speech I had planned before Carter rang the doorbell, but I had been thinking about what I wanted to say to Ash all night on the patio. I knew I had one chance to get this right.

"I know this messes everything up. That you're not ready for them to know. That we need to keep things under wraps for the next week. But please, Ashy, don't make any decisions until we can talk this through. Don't end things for good without giving me a say."

Ash opened his mouth and closed it several times, like the protest was ready on his tongue but didn't quite make it out.

"Okay," he finally promised, his word no more than a breath.

I let out a noiseless sigh, the worry in my chest temporarily lessening.

"Okay," I repeated. The ghost of a smile appeared on his lips. Lips that I had grown to know so well recently.

Not wanting to press my luck, I quickly gathered my things. I peered out to check that the coast was clear before sneaking back across the hall after closing Ash's door behind me. The walk to my own room was only five steps, but I froze halfway when another bedroom door opened. Jamie stepped into the hallway, toothbrush in one hand, toothpaste in the other. His jaw dropped as he noticed my suitcase, clearly coming out of Ash's room. I shot him a warning look, and fortunately he had the good grace to keep quiet, but any chance of him not knowing what was going on between Ash and me was eliminated in that damning moment.

I lay awake for a long time that night. The sheets were too blue, not crisp white like the ones in Ash's room. The pillows were too firm. The bed was too large, too empty, too cold. My thoughts were too loud. I tossed and turned, unable to drift off without Ashy's steady deep breaths beside me.

Fucking Carter, man. I swear he was the mastermind behind this little surprise. It was totally like him to cockblock me. He was probably sleeping peacefully next door with his big stupid arms wrapped around his perfect, tiny fiancé—dreaming of sugarplums or guitar riffs or something equally boring and wholesome—none the wiser to the chaos his early presence had created.

I must have eventually fallen asleep because the next thing I knew, the smell of coffee and bacon woke me up. My stomach grumbled as I got up and dressed. I came downstairs to the kitchen to find Papa Ash busy at the stove, splitting his attention between the bacon, eggs, and pancakes he was cooking. Beau was setting the dining table.

"Hey, thought I'd cook a big breakfast before we get started with rehearsal," Ash said, spatula in hand.

"Smells fantastic," I said.

Wanting to help, I slid behind Ash to grab a jug of orange juice out of the fridge. It was a well-choreographed dance we had done numerous times in the small kitchen since we'd began living together. As I shuffled to the cupboard to grab the glasses, I froze a split second before automatically putting my hand on his waist. It was so unconscious now, touching him. I shook my head to clear it, moving on and grabbing six tumblers for the juice.

"Morning," Chase said from the bottom of the stairs. Carter followed him faithfully.

"Morning!" Ash answered. "Breakfast is two minutes away. Coffee's on the counter." He gestured to the full pot.

"Anyone seen Jam-Jam yet?" I asked.

Beau and Ash gestured to the backyard at the same time. I looked out the window, and sure enough, Jamie was outside doing some crazy-stretchy yoga pose in the middle of the grass.

I chuckled. "How long's he been there?"

"Was out there when I came downstairs," Ash said with a shrug.

"He was up before me," Beau added.

Seeing an opportunity to get Jamie alone, I nobly sacrificed first dibs on the pancakes to help reassure my guy nobody was going to spill the proverbial beans. "I'll go grab him."

Ash

PEERING inconspicuously out the kitchen window, I observed Jamie seemingly defy gravity in a headstand on the back lawn. How much did he know? He wouldn't say anything, would he?

Dean went running down the hill toward him, arms out to his sides like an airplane, screaming like a banshee. So much for Jamie's peaceful yoga time.

Jamie fell out of the position he was in, lightly shoving Dean in the chest when he righted himself. It looked like they were both laughing, thankfully. I returned my attention to the food and flipped the last of the pancakes off the grill. I was no Cherie Phillips with the breakfast skills, but it was edible. Carter helped me carry everything to the table. I took my usual chair, which faced toward the window and gave me a prime view of Jamie and Dean, who were making no move to come toward the house.

"Should we wait for them?" Chase asked, nodding outside.

"Nah," I said. "I'm sure they'll be in in a minute. Eat it while it's hot."

Conversation soared around me, though I could barely focus on any of it. I tried to keep my glances out the window subtle, desperate to know what Dean was saying to Jamie. Would he need to confirm we were together to get Jamie to keep quiet? Would he be typical Dean and brush off the importance of the whole thing? I watched Jamie burst out laughing at something Dean said. Were they mocking how into the sex I was?

Were they even talking about me at all?

I was being fucking paranoid. At the very least, Dean was my best friend, and I trusted him to respect my wishes. I forced myself to listen to whatever Carter was saying instead of trying to interpret the conversation I was not privy to.

"...or we'll rent out a larger space and make it a huge party. Haven't decided yet," Carter said.

"As long as we're both there and you look hot as fuck in your suit, the details don't matter," Chase added. Beau laughed along with the two of them.

My gaze floated back outside to where Jamie had his arm around Dean's shoulders. They were closer now, slowly making their way back to the house. Dean looked up and met my eyes through the window. He winked at me, and my cheeks heated, knowing I'd been caught staring. I fuddled my way back to my breakfast. The scrambled eggs were like rubber on my tongue.

"Oh, there you are," Beau said as Jamie and Dean strolled through the sliding door. Jamie kissed Beau's head as he pulled out the chair next to his boyfriend.

"Sorry," Jamie said. "Lost track of time. It's so relaxing to be able to do yoga outside here. I may need to find a place with a proper backyard when we go back home."

"A backyard big enough for yoga? In Manhattan? Good luck," Dean scoffed as he took a bite of one of the pieces of bacon he was double fisting. "You should totally move here instead. New York has nothing on Amberwood. Clean air. Lots of space. Good food."

"Might make for a shitty commute to work at Juilliard, though," Jamie mused. "Though it would be easier to get a dog out here in the country."

I watched the two of them in amusement. Lord knows how, but the unlikely pair of Jamie and Dean had become such good friends over the course of the European tour. It was nice to see them reconnect, no matter how nervous it made me.

"Ohhh, Ashy! We should totally get a dog!" Dean's eyes were wide with excitement.

"No." I shook my head.

"Come on! I promise I'll take care of it."

"What happens when we go out on tour again? Your mom wouldn't be able to look after a dog with her hours at the diner."

"Then it could live with your parents. Come on, Ashy, it would be so much fun! Pleassse?"

I rolled my eyes at him.

"You know who's got the sweetest dog?" Dean went on, pouting at me and talking to the rest of the group. "Jasmine, the woman I told you about. Who runs the center? Her dog, Bella, is the bestest girl."

Dean enthused about Jasmine and Bella and all things Indigo House for the rest of breakfast. On the one hand, I remained immensely proud of everything Dean was doing for the program and for the kids. On the other, I was irrationally jealous of the way Dean went on and on about Jasmine. I knew it was ridiculous. I had no claim over Dean, and no reason to assume he was even attracted to the pretty Indigo House director. But it remained a sore spot. More than anything, I wanted to do something that made Dean equally proud.

Twenty minutes later, Dean and I were cleaning up in the kitchen while everyone else was helping to unload instruments and gear in the living room for the rehearsal. My skin was still crawling, and I was probably banging the dishes and cutlery around harder than necessary.

In all the years I'd known Dean, I'd never felt like we were so out of sync.

"You okay over there, growly?" Dean asked quietly.

"I'm fine," I said shortly.

"She's just a friend," he repeated for the thousandth time.

Carter walked into the kitchen and paused, looking between the two of us and undoubtedly sensing the tension.

"Hey, um, we're all set up in there when you guys are ready to start," Carter said.

Honestly I wasn't even sure why I was so pissed off. Deep down I knew Dean wasn't interested in Jasmine. It was more that Jasmine was sweet and successful and the kind of person Dean would normally go for. And by that I meant a woman. Dean didn't really have a type beyond that.

Jasmine had no reason not to flirt with Dean. He had a reputation, and she would have no indication to think she was offending me by it. From being around her, I knew she was a good person and certainly wouldn't blatantly hit on him in front of me if she knew we were… whatever we were.

I wished I was as comfortable with all this as Dean seemed to be. Comfortable enough to tell my parents. Comfortable enough to tell Jasmine to fuck off, that he was *my* man. Comfortable enough to claim him in front of anyone and everyone. At the very least, comfortable enough to believe what he'd told me last night. That things were just on pause between us while the band was here, that we would talk after.

Although I was still pissed off, I pushed the last cupboard door closed slightly less forcefully than I would have a minute ago.

"Yup. Let's go." I headed toward the den, leaving Carter and Dean behind.

Nobody ever said love was rational.

Dean

THE new song Carter and Chase wrote fucking rocked. The beat rocked. The lyrics rocked. The band *fucking rocked* when we played it.

I could practically smell awards season jizzing all over us.

It was everything Carter had originally described it as and more. It was a fight song. It was an anthem. It was a generational call to arms. An LGBTQ+ battle cry. A song of passion and love and rage. Our second album was good; it did well on the charts, and I could honestly say I was proud of the shit on it. But we hadn't had a song this magical since "Next to Me." "Stained Glass Cathedrals and Chantilly Lace" was going to skyrocket the Thorns.

The more we played it over the following three days, the more certain I was that this was our bolt of lightning. It kept getting better with each pass. Every time I was certain it was perfect, Carter would throw in a fresh riff, Beau would change a single chord slightly, or Ash would try a different pass with the cymbals, and my mind was blown yet again. The talent surrounding me was insane. I knew musically I wasn't even close to the level of the other three Thorns, but goddamn I was happy to be along for the ride.

As good as things were with the band, the tension between Ash and me grew with each day of rehearsal. He stubbornly refused to be alone with me. We had agreed to put things on pause, but it didn't need to be this way. The band knew we were friends. Right now he wasn't even allowing us to be that. It hurt. Every conversation we had included other members of the group, and they were mostly catering to the class-clown expectation everyone had of me. I didn't dare bring up Indigo House or Jasmine again out of fear for making things worse.

This horrible stalemate between Ash and me—the poignant looks, the polite, surface-level conversations—made me ache for the real him. The miles of distance between our two neighboring bedrooms seemed to increase every night.

On the first morning of the band's visit, I had made sure Jamie hadn't discussed what I had told him on the phone with anyone. He reassured me he wouldn't do that to me and then proceeded to push for gossip about what had happened since. Jamie saw me sneak out of Ash's room, so complete denial seemed in poor taste. As a compromise, I had been evasive; not lying outright, but respectful of Ash's wishes not to say anything. I hoped that would be enough.

It was weird to keep something from the band. Ash reacted so strongly I knew there was more to it than he was letting on. The worst part was I didn't understand *why* it was such a huge deal to tell them. To tell our families. I mean, I got that Ash was scared—this was big and new and different. But his family were all great people; I couldn't see a scenario where they would be upset by this. And the band! Carter and Beau were both in same-sex relationships. They were our best friends, our brothers through this insane life we had created together. They would unquestionably be our biggest supporters. Like we were for them.

I was at a loss. It hurt that Ash put up this wall between us. If he would just *talk* to me, I could be his partner and help him through whatever was bugging him. The longer we went without talking, the more I second-guessed things. The longer he had to overthink, the higher the chances were he would decide it wasn't worth it after all.

It was two days before the concert, the final afternoon of rehearsing in Ash's house before we moved to the stage in Boston. The set the Thorns had created was becoming tight. It was basically a mix of our greatest hits, plus the one new song. In our standard band positioning, Carter was front and center and Beau was to the left of him. Ash was behind Beau—taking up most of the real estate with his large drum kit—and I hung out in the back right. Naturally, Ash and I spent most of the show looking at Carter's and Beau's backs and fell directly into each other's line of sight. While we were completely an equal-partners foursome, it had always been Beau and Carter, and Ash and me. The melody duo and the rhythm section.

I snuck a peek at Ash. The angst he had carried around me lately was gone, and he had this dopey grin on his face. Ash had a natural ease when he played music. He was born to do this. If he hadn't played drums for Thorns, he would be playing the violin for the Boston Symphony with his parents or something else equally as impressive. I'd gotten him involved in Heartbeat with Indigo House because he was not only the most talented guy I knew, but also the most passionate.

More than anything, I wanted Ashy to be happy. I knew in my heart I could give that to him. He just needed to let me.

Ash

AFTER the final day of rehearsal at my house, we decided to have a cookout. Tomorrow we were all driving up to Boston and spending a couple of nights in a hotel close to the venue, so none of us needed to worry about commuting back and forth to Amberwood. I made an army's worth of grilled chicken—veggie substitutes for Beau—and all sorts of toppings and sides. We lit a bonfire in the firepit and roasted marshmallows and laughed late into the night.

The festivities began to wind down around midnight, with Carter and Chase deciding to call it quits. Dean followed shortly after, as he had procrastinated packing for the road trip.

"Are you doing okay, Ash?" Beau asked after he, Jamie, and I had been staring into the fire for a while in silence. "You've been off since we got here."

He was right. Though I had tried to hide it, the Thorns knew me so well it didn't surprise me Beau had picked up that something was wrong. I sighed.

I had made such a big deal to Dean about not telling the band, it would be wrong to go and blurt it out to Beau. It was a decision we should be making together. I couldn't say anything.

"Hey, babe, why don't you head up to bed?" Jamie said to his boyfriend gently. Beau looked at him, confused. Jamie nodded reassuringly; a whole conversation passed between the two wordlessly. Finally Beau nodded.

"I'll be up soon," Jamie told Beau, kissing him quickly.

Beau pressed his hands to his knees and stood to leave. He clapped my shoulder on his way past, undoubtedly wondering what the hell was going on but trusting Jamie had things under control. I wanted that. A partner to rely on.

Jamie poked the fire absently with the long stick he had been using to toast marshmallows. Once we heard the sliding door close behind Beau, Jamie cleared his throat.

"So, um, I have this friend. His name is… Dale—"

I sighed, not having the energy to play cute or coy.

"I know Dean told you," I said. My tone was straight, with no anger or animosity behind it. Simple fact. The weather is nice. That song was good. I know you know.

"He didn't say much," Jamie admitted.

While I didn't know Jamie particularly well, he had gotten close to Dean. I trusted him to be discreet. It didn't seem like he had gone blabbing to Beau or anyone else after Dean talked to him, so I figured it was safe enough. A calculated risk. I took a chance and filled Jamie in on the gist: the post-*Grammy* threesome, the first time Dean and I had hooked up after returning to Amberwood, the subsequent affair. I told him how I freaked out after the initial encounter. How I figured out that I was gay. How Dean wasn't as serious about this as I was, but I couldn't seem to end things between us. How right it felt to me.

I talked for an hour, or it seemed like it. I went from defeated, to angry, to nostalgic. I laughed in memory of the good times and got caught up in the romance of how sweet Dean could be. It was cathartic to tell someone such a weighty secret. I got why it had burdened Dean to keep it all inside. Jamie listened to every word. He reacted to what I said but let me get everything off my chest without interruption.

When I was finally done, I sighed and relaxed. For the first time in two months, I was able to take a deep breath.

"Wow," Jamie said eventually. "That's a lot. Thank you for telling me. Can I ask something, though?"

I nodded, suddenly exhausted by the intensity of the conversation and the late hour.

"How do you know Dean's not serious?" Jamie asked. "Because nothing you said seems to imply that he's not."

"'Cause he's Dean," I replied, gesturing widely with my hands as if that was enough to explain Dean's entire personality. "He's not serious about anything. He likes groupies. One-night stands. Women."

"Listen," Jamie started and then paused to poke at the fire again. "You know Deano better than I ever will. You guys go back more than a decade. You have a bond that is totally unique. Totally *you*. But I think you're putting him in a box here. Yeah, he's a pretty laid-back guy most of the time, but he's *exceedingly* determined when he wants to be."

Jamie looked at me poignantly, and my stomach lurched as I considered what he was saying.

"Dean practiced ballet for *four months* to pull off a stupid ten-second joke," Jamie went on. "He started an entire music program at a kids center when he wanted to help. Not only did he learn to play the bass with no formal training—without being able to read music, I might add—but he plays well enough to be in the biggest rock band out there right now. Dean can be a fucking serious guy when he wants to be."

Absorbing Jamie's words, I blinked rapidly. I watched the fire, the dark red embers as they crackled and popped into the night. Jamie was right. The point about the center had been something I had thought about a lot lately, but the other two examples I had previously brushed off. Considering it now, they were pretty damn incredible feats Dean had pulled off. He hadn't grown up with a lot of opportunities, but Dean was the glue of the Thorns. Maybe none of us had been giving him enough credit.

Jamie touched my arm gently before continuing. "What you guys have going on has lasted way longer than one of his ridiculous groupie encounters. He admires you, Ash. He brags to anyone who will listen about how talented you are with your music. It doesn't seem like an experiment for him from anything you've told me."

I let out a long, stuttering breath.

I knew what I wanted. I had known from the beginning. Being with Dean had seemed so impossible, but we were doing it. We had been for months. I had been pushing him away lately to protect myself, because it didn't feel like I had any other option.

Later that night, when I was alone in bed, I thought more about what Jamie had said. I hadn't stopped thinking about it, if I was being honest. Dean had been trying to say something to me right before Carter and the rest of the guys barged in. It certainly hadn't sounded trivial, and he had a hard time getting it out. At the time I had brushed it off, assuming he was simply saying the right things to get laid. But now I realized it wasn't that. I'd kind of been a dick to him lately, avoiding what I thought would be an inevitable conclusion for us.

Self-preservation.

Fear.

Dean and I were opposites in almost every way. I had so many opportunities growing up, and he had so few. He had deep, meaningful relationships with friends, and I was likely to push people away. I relied on orderly written music, and he made his parts up on the fly. He was impulsive, easygoing, and lighthearted. He was beautiful. He made everyone around him laugh.

He led with his heart, not his head.

When I was with Dean, he made me less fearful. More self-confident. Freer.

Maybe I finally needed to let myself jump.

Slowly, silently, I got out of my bed and crept into the deserted hallway. I opened Dean's door. He stirred in his sleep but didn't open his eyes. I climbed into my guest bed and pulled the covers over my shoulders.

"Hey," he said. His voice was raspy and confused.

Dean turned over slightly and looked at me, ran his fingers along my jaw.

I wrapped my arms around his warm body in the unfamiliar bed. For the first time in four nights, I was exactly where I was supposed to be. Leaning in, I kissed the spot below his ear before I whispered, "Shh, go back to sleep."

Dean

ON the day of the Boston concert technical rehearsal, I fought waking up from the best dream I'd had in a long time. I'd dreamt that in the middle of the night, Ashy had snuck into my room and held me. It was wonderful. It felt so real. Even now I could practically hear his soft snores. Sense the warmth of his arm around me. Smell the sandalwood that lingered on his skin. Feel his thick morning wood pressing against my ass.

Wait.

My eyes snapped open from a shot of adrenaline in my veins. Keeping my body completely stationary, I looked around quickly as I took in the now-familiar surroundings of Ash's guest room. Tentatively, I wiggled my hips backward to see if this was all a figment of my very imaginative imagination. The hardness against my ass thrust back against me.

Nope. The very rigid dick was definitely not imaginary.

I weighed my options.

Still mostly asleep, Ash moaned against the back of my neck.

The unbelievably erogenous sound made my choice obvious.

Gradually, so as not to shock him and risk him yelling out, I began to grind backward. It was sleepy and slow. The perfect way to start what would be a long day. Ash woke up more against me. He burrowed his face into my hair and tightened his hold on my hip. I pushed the pajama pants he wore down; the blazing heat of his cock was amazing against my bare skin. Even though I had no idea what was going on—why he was in my bed, why he was suddenly okay with this—I was too far gone to question it. We didn't have much time, and we had to be completely silent, but it was all too good to resist. I would have to thank Ashy later for his prudent investment in the expensive nonsqueaky bedframe.

He shifted positions so his cock was between my thighs. His thrusts gained intensity. It was far sexier than I would have thought, arousing the delicate skin along my taint and balls. The friction was almost too much without lube, but who were we kidding? There was no way either of us was going to last.

"Fuck, Dean," he growled in my ear.

The move shot me closer to my impending orgasm; his breath on my sensitive ears always did me in. He reached around to jerk me off at the same time.

"You're so fucking sexy. God, your body turns me on. Missed it so much. Wanna be inside you so bad right now," he told me.

I whimpered, unable to stop myself.

This was different. We'd never talked much during sex in the past, beyond the occasional moan or vocalization—this was new for us. I liked it. I *really* liked it.

Ash's thrusts grew more erratic, his breathing more strained. With one last groan, he covered my balls and thighs with his seed. Through his orgasm, he continued to lick and nibble at my neck and ear, mixing sweet kisses with dirty promises. After a few more perfect strokes, the world fell apart under me as Ash's strong hands held me safe.

I lay there as the room slowly came back into focus. I became aware of what we had done and why that was confusing after the past few days. Bracing myself, I rolled over, prepared for the inevitable "I need to sneak out of this room so nobody knows" speech. But that didn't happen. Ash stroked my cheeks. He tucked my hair behind my ear. He kissed my bottom lip. Just when I was about to ask what the hell was going on, he spoke first.

"I wanna take you to dinner tonight. After soundcheck. Only you and me. Figure things out."

I balked in what was surely an unattractive way. My natural instinct was to deflect, make a joke, or brush off Ash's sincerity. He kissed me again, and all humor was sucked out of the room.

"O-okay," I stuttered, looking into his eyes, searching for clues as to what was going on. What the catch was.

Ash smirked like he was going to tease me, but the alarm on my phone interrupted the moment.

"Guess that means we've gotta get up." Ash stretched his long arms over his head, momentarily distracting me with the miles of bare skin on display.

"You just made me come my brains out, Ashy. I'm gonna need a few minutes before I can go again."

He swatted my ass at the bad joke. "Let's go."

Dean

AFTER getting out of bed, Ash and I showered separately and dressed quickly, then joined the guys for breakfast before the road trip. We had gone back to our status quo around the rest of the group for the day—an unspoken decision. However, there was noticeably less tension between us. We teased each other like usual and exchanged more under-the-radar flirty looks. I wasn't sure exactly what had changed, but I was less paranoid about the others picking up on the transformation between us.

We drove up to Boston in two vehicles. Ash drove his car, which Carter and I rode in, and Beau, Jamie, and Chase went in Beau's rental. After the concert, the other four would head back to New York while Ash and I returned to Amberwood. It was only an hour or so in the car, and there was plenty to talk about without things getting awkward.

The technical rehearsal went fantastically. Maybe it was the time apart, maybe it was because of the stress-free band practice over the past few days, or maybe it was because of the relatively simple stage setup, but it was one of the smoothest soundcheck days we'd had. When we were packing up our gear, I looked over and locked eyes with Ashy, shooting him a smile for everything to come. Ash headed into the wings, carrying one of the large cymbals he was disassembling.

"Dean?" I turned around to where the voice was coming from. "Oh hey, I thought that was you!"

"Maddy?" I squinted my eyes to take in the gorgeous woman in front of me I hadn't seen since the night of the *Grammy Awards*.

I jogged down the two steps of the stage deck to meet her in the front row of seats. She wrapped her arms around me in a friendly hug.

"What are you doing here?" I asked.

"My stepbrother, Brent, is actually drumming with your opening band. Their regular drummer broke his hand, and they needed a last-minute replacement. Heard it was gonna be a great show, and I talked myself into a ticket." She giggled easily.

She wasn't flirty the way she had been on the night back in LA, for which I was grateful. Maddy was beautiful, but nothing about her sparked my interest anymore. I gazed back at the stage, where Ash was bent over—ass in the air—pulling apart another piece of his drum kit. My mouth watered at the visual. Yep, only one person stole my attention these days.

Maddy followed my line of sight.

"I take it you two figured things out, then?" She tilted her head in Ash's direction.

"What?" I asked, furrowing my brow.

"You and Ash? You're staring at him like he's the gold at the end of the rainbow."

"Oh." I turned my attention back to her as my cheeks heated. Embarrassment won out for a second before I couldn't help but add, "Maybe he is."

I shook my head to clear it of my Ash-induced fog, focusing on Maddy's words. "Wait. What do you mean we figured it out? We weren't together back then."

Maddy scoffed. "Maybe not, but you clearly wanted to be. I've never felt so much like a third wheel in my life. I'd give anything to have a guy look at me like you were looking at each other."

I thought back to the night of the *Grammys*. It hadn't been that long ago, but it felt like another lifetime. I remembered proposing the hookup to Ashy and him being hesitant at first. I remembered the heat, the sweat, the intertwining limbs. I remembered focusing on Maddy... until that one moment.

That one moment I'd played off as an accident, but it couldn't have been more real. Perhaps it began as a mistake, a split second where my hand was supposed to land on her thigh but found his instead. There was no mistaking her petite, smooth leg for his powerful, masculine one. Once the realization hit, I could have changed course, corrected. But I didn't. I wanted it to be him I was touching, even if in that moment I didn't understand why.

And I guess there may have been some other things too. I may have stolen a look at him once or twice. At his body. His face. His cock. I'd never thought about Ashy like that before, but I couldn't deny I was curious in the moment when the opportunity presented itself. Ash wasn't at all like the movie stars you see on TV.

His stomach was not quite flat and didn't boast any visible abs. His chest was scattered with coarse dark hair, and his fingers were calloused. I'd never been turned on by the movie guys, although my reaction to Ash was evident.

The night might have started by my wanting to be with Maddy, but it was my hand on Ashy's leg that made me come.

I assumed it was a one-off. A random occurrence and a coincidence of timing. Thinking back on it now, I knew it was more than that. It was my body—my soul—knowing the truth months before my brain did. If Maddy, a perfect stranger, had realized it that night, the whole thing must have been pretty damn obvious.

At that moment, Ash looked over from what he was doing onstage. He gave me a bright smile when he met my gaze. When he noticed who I was with, he froze. I winked at him, trying to convey that everything was fine and he had nothing to worry about.

Maddy noticed the interaction and graciously took a step away from me.

"I'm sorry," I said. "Believe me, that wasn't my intention. I guess Ashy just… distracts me. Even if I didn't realize it at the time."

She smiled at me with far more kindness than I deserved. "No hard feelings. It wasn't like I really lost that night, having two Thorns in my bed."

We laughed together and caught up for a few more minutes. I was grateful she was so relaxed about the whole thing. She had been looking for sex that night, nothing further. No epic romance for the ages. No fairy-tale ending. I recognized it because it was how I used to do things. How I had operated for years. But casual hookups weren't for me any longer. I wanted so much more than that. I wanted the love story.

Covering my bases, I made sure to ask Maddy to keep quiet on the topic of me and Ash. She agreed with a sad, understanding smile. Eventually Maddy made her way back over to the other band, who were finishing the setup for their own soundcheck.

I found Ash when he was locking up the last of his gear.

"Hey," I said.

It was a funny feeling, the butterflies. I'd known Ashy forever. I'd seen his awkward years, his struggles with self-confidence, and his rise to fame. I'd watched him drink himself stupid, puke when he got tattooed, and cry out of homesickness on our first tour. Yet it was like I was seeing him with new eyes. We'd already slept together, already *lived* together. But the prospect of our first real date made me wobbly.

"Hey," he responded. His smile looked as nervous as I felt.

I took a deep breath. "You ready to go?"

Ash

SEEING Dean with Maddy after soundcheck immediately made me jealous. But after he smiled at me, it was clear I had nothing to worry about.

I'd had no idea what to do on a date with not just a guy, but a guy like Dean. Romantic candlelight and soufflé for dessert would be stuffy, and the added stress of remembering which forks to use was *so* not what I needed tonight. Plus there was the factor that while I didn't get recognized in public frequently, he did. As grateful as we both were to have fans, this conversation was too important to have in public and risk being interrupted.

After successfully ditching the others without too many questions, I swiped my key card and let us into the hotel room. I'd called ahead this morning and upgraded my room to a larger suite, complete with a wraparound private balcony. On the balcony was a patio table with two chairs and our meal already laid out for us.

"What the hell, Ashy? My room's the size of a strawberry compared to this place."

I tried to keep a straight face as I sat down at the table and began uncovering the plates of food. "What? Cory doesn't give you penthouse suites when we're on the road? To be honest this is a little basic for what I normally get, but what can you do?"

He looked at me like he was trying to figure out if I was screwing with him. I broke and cracked a smile, unable to keep up the charade.

"Kidding. Wanted some space for us tonight, so I called in some favors." I handed him a beer and gestured to the burgers in front of us. "Figured this was better than fancy people food."

"Absolutely," Dean said as he took a seat. "This chick I went out with once ordered some sort of foam fish bullshit, thought it was classy or something. I got roasted chicken, and I'm pretty sure she ate three-quarters of it 'cause hers was so nasty."

I held up my burger to his in a toast. "To no bullshit."

We ate for a few minutes in silence. I had planned what I wanted to tell him through the afternoon, now it was just about finding the balls to actually say it.

"So," Dean started, opening the conversation neutrally.

I took a deep breath to steady my nerves. "I'm... gay," I said.

My voice sounded strange in my ears. There it was. I'd said it.

Dean got up from his chair without a word. He gently took my hand off my glass and pulled me up. His arms wrapped around me, and he held me tight. It felt right. It was comforting and tender and exactly what I needed in the moment. After my heart stopped racing, he pulled back and cupped my jaw, kissing me once before sitting back down at the table. He kept hold of my left hand, stroking his thumb over my knuckles.

"Is that something you've known for a while?" he finally asked.

I shook my head. "No. Maybe? I'd had suspicions, but I didn't know for sure until we...." I gestured abstractly, letting him fill in the blanks.

Dean nodded solemnly like he understood.

"My ass made you gay. I knew it was a good ass, but—"

I backhanded his chest playfully. "Shut up. You know what I meant."

Dean laughed and grabbed my hand again, kissing it before returning to our previous position.

It was a wonderful sound, his laugh.

I didn't correct him on specifics, knowing it didn't make much difference that I had figured it out for sure during our first time on the sofa. No asses involved— not even any nudity. Dean had been the catalyst, and I was finally able to tell him so. That's what mattered.

"I guess I've been struggling since that night in LA. Maybe even before that," I went on. "It changed something in me. Or made me think about it for the first time, I guess. I just... I want to know what you think because this is a really big fucking deal for me, and I have no idea where you're at."

My words came out faster and faster, squeaky and bordering on panicked. Dean stared at me intently.

"I'm sorry," I said after taking a breath to calm myself. "Maybe this is all coming out wrong."

"I think you're coming out just fine," Dean said. His slight alteration to my words calmed me for some reason. I knew I was accepted. Whatever happened he would stand by me. At least as a friend.

"I never told you what I said to Jamie on the phone that day," Dean continued casually. "Right after we got back from the tour."

I shook my head, unsure about exactly where this was going. His call with Jamie had caused such a big fight, I wasn't sure I wanted to revisit that, but it seemed important to him that he tell me.

"I called Jamie because I was panicking. For the first time in my life, I'd found myself attracted to a guy. Not just a guy, but *my* guy. My best friend. My Ash. I didn't know what to do, what to think. I told Jamie.... I told Jamie that I was in love with you."

My eyes went wide and everything stopped. The air caught in my lungs; the noise of the evening traffic faded to silence. The overactive pounding of my heart was the only sign the world continued to spin around me.

Dean let out a nervous puff of air and pushed his curls off his forehead. "And yeah, maybe I was being a little dramatic."

A single laugh caught in my throat. This was important, but it was so Dean I couldn't help but react. I slowly let out the breath I had been holding, needing him to continue before I went crazy.

"But that doesn't stop it from being true," he said softly. "I think I've been falling in love with you for fifteen years. I just didn't know it."

The prickling behind my eyes and the cantaloupe-sized knot in my throat made it difficult to respond. I'm pretty sure Dean kept talking—something about my bodywash, experimenting with gay porn, not labeling himself—but nothing really registered. His words were fast, but his eyes were sincere.

"It was never an experiment for me," Dean concluded. "I know you think I'm all about easy sex and getting off, but I promise that's never what this has been. I wouldn't risk our friendship for something that shallow. From the first time with you, Ashy, I've always wanted more."

He looked at me expectantly. It was so dumb; I was the one who had started this conversation, and he had done most of the important talking. For some reason I still couldn't force myself to form words. It was all too much.

I wasn't sure exactly what I'd expected from tonight, whether I'd entirely trusted what Jamie told me by the fire, or whether I was secretly preparing myself for the worst. But Dean's sincerity and heartfelt words were a lot to process.

"Please, Ashy, say something? Tell me what you think. Tell me you feel the same way?"

It was like leaping off a massive cliff. No running start, no looking cautiously over the edge. Just a whispered prayer and a blind jump. Sort of like the first time Dean and I hooked up.

Only this time, I was positive he would catch me.

"I love you too."

Dean

I HAD always been a fuck-and-run kinda guy, never really gave a shit about a hookup after the clothes were back on. Relationships? Not a chance. Throwing everything out there and waiting for Ash to tell me how he felt was the most terrifying thing I'd ever done in my life.

And also the most freeing.

Like, even if Ash told me he didn't feel the same way, I wouldn't regret saying what I did. Because at least then he would know, right?

I wanted him to know.

"I love you too," Ash said with the shy smile he only ever used on me.

The stupidly large grin on my face was instant. Possibly before the words had even fully left his mouth.

I slid my chair back, moved to his, and straddled him. He gasped a little in surprise but quickly locked his arms around my waist, holding me steady. It was intimate as hell with the two of us so close. His lap was warm and solid. I could feel his heartbeat, the goose bumps that dotted his skin. I shifted closer, my lips a breath away. His arousal grew against me, but I ignored it.

"Tell me again," I whispered.

Ash shuddered. His Adam's apple bobbed in his throat. "I love you too," he responded, less tentatively this time.

I took his lips in a ravaging kiss, pouring every ounce of passion and desire and lust I had into it. He gave as good as he got, wrapping his hands around my neck to control my movements. My tongue pushed into his mouth. It was messy and chaotic. The stubble on his cheeks scraped against me, abrading my skin in the most delicious way. There was no hesitation between us anymore. No tentative touches or moments of indecision. Only pure want.

He drove me higher and higher, sucking on my tongue and moaning into my mouth. His hands slid down and palmed my ass, groping and clawing with need. I'd never felt so desired in my life. Nothing and nobody came anywhere close to Ash.

Without warning he stood up from under me. My legs wrapped tightly around his hips as his strong biceps strained under my weight. I buried my face in his neck as he carried me inside. Thank fuck the bed was close because I think I would have spontaneously combusted if I had to wait any longer. Ash tossed me onto the bed as if I weighed nothing. He stripped his shirt off quickly before lying on top of me. Chest to chest. Legs to legs. Hips to hips.

I lost myself in him. In his kisses. His touches. His thrusts. Each moment was heightened, and every second became better than the last. We spent the night in each other's arms, alternating between making love and talking about anything and everything. We laughed and we joked and most importantly, we were still *us*. I had never been as connected to anyone, so at peace with myself.

When the sun finally began to rise, he turned to kiss me leisurely, exhausted from God knows how many rounds and not nearly enough sleep.

"I want to tell people," Ash said. He ran his fingers through my hair like he did so frequently.

"Hmm?" I mumbled, half-asleep.

"I want to tell people. About us. I'm ready."

I woke up a little, and his words sank in. Ash had told me last night that he hadn't wanted anyone to know because he was scared I wasn't serious. Would hurt him and leave him to deal with the aftermath. Him wanting to tell people was a massive sign of trust in me and in our relationship. I was so proud of Ashy for everything he was and all he accomplished; this made me love him a little bit more.

"Today?" I asked.

He chuckled at my enthusiasm.

"Maybe not today, but soon. I want my parents to know first. And the band."

"Carter's gonna flip his shit when he finds out." I laughed. "We should just start making out in front of him one day. See what happens."

Ash snorted loudly. "He'd probably think it was only another one of your jokes."

"I am *all* for committing for the sake of the reaction." I raised one eyebrow. "Hell, I'd probably get away with having half your dick down my throat before he figured out we were being serious."

"For the record, in front of our friends would be one of the few times I would ever turn down your mouth on me. I don't share you. Not anymore."

"Oh really?" I challenged, ignoring the swoony feeling in my stomach. "What about on stage in front of a sold-out crowd at Wembley Stadium? Would you turn me down then?"

Ash shook his head. "If they let us play there, there's no way in hell I'm fucking it up."

"Fine. What about in an underground leather-and-lace sex club?"

"I think we're a little too well known for that."

"Of course noooow you wanna play the rock star card," I scoffed. "What about… hmmm."

I paused to think of another outrageous scenario to continue teasing him. "What about in one of those tiny airplane bathrooms where everyone knows exactly what you're doing but nobody can prove it?"

Ash automatically began shaking his head, but a slight moan gave him away once he digested my words. His cock twitched against my leg. I smirked to myself as I knew I'd won this little game.

I crawled down his body, leaving a trail of kisses in my wake. His cock was still mostly soft as I took the tip into my mouth.

"Goddammit, Dean. I've already come a million times tonight. There's nothing left—" Ash cut off his words with a moan as I took him deep.

Ash growing harder in my mouth was incredibly sexy. I smiled around his dick as it continued to swell slowly.

"Fuck, baby," he said. "This is going to fucking hurt. Don't you dare stop."

Dean

"WHERE the hell were you last night?" Carter asked. "I knocked on your door like three separate times."

The opening band had just finished their set—and killed it, I might add—so there was a lot of anticipation building in the short time it took the stage crew to turn over our gear. We were waiting in the wings, ready for Jasmine to introduce us. The venue was packed—not a seat was left empty—and donations in addition to ticket revenue were through the roof. All in all, the fundraiser was an overwhelming success for Indigo House.

"I, um," I stuttered, looking around frantically for Ash. We had talked a little about how he wanted to tell the rest of the guys but distracted ourselves before any official decision was made. I was a notoriously bad actor, and lying to Carter wouldn't get me far. However, there was no way I was telling him the truth without Ashy's input.

"Ash and I hung out. Got some food and beers in his room." All technically true. Carter wouldn't see anything out of the ordinary there or assume anything more happened. No need to tell him the reason why I was in Ash's suite or what happened after said dinner and drinks.

Carter studied me for a second without saying anything. He nodded with a funny look in his eye. The back of my neck tingled. Carter opened his mouth to speak, but fortunately Jasmine chose that moment to walk up to us.

"Hey, you guys ready?" she asked.

"Hecks yes we are!" I said enthusiastically, pushing aside the weird vibe with Carter.

"Thank you guys again for doing this," Jasmine said. "I literally don't know how we'll ever repay you. We were in such a tight spot before, and this concert has completely turned things around."

"Just keep the music program going. That's all the thanks we need. And I'll never say no to hearing about how the kids are doing," I told her sincerely.

"Absolutely," Jasmine agreed.

"Hey, we on soon?" Ash asked, strolling up with Beau. Ash kept his distance from me, like we had been doing all afternoon. A few days ago that would have bothered me, but now I knew it was temporary, and we would tell the rest of the Thorns soon enough. Carter stared at Ash with a strange look.

Beau glanced out into the packed audience, pointing to them with his thumb. "Good crowd out there. Hey, um, Deano, has Cory found you yet? He wanted to see you before we go on."

"No," I said, furrowing my brow. "Why would he wanna see me?"

"I dunno…." Beau wavered like he knew exactly why Cory was looking for me but didn't want to say.

Why were Carter and Beau both acting so weird today?

"You've got, like, five minutes," Carter said. "Better go track him down."

I looked between them, unsure what was up. Glancing into the back corner, I saw Cory talking to one of the stage crew. I left the group and walked toward him, feeling everyone's eyes on me.

"Oh, good," Cory said as I approached. "Lots of kids in the crowd tonight. Wanna make sure we keep things… professional."

"Got it," I said, rolling my eyes at the lecture from our grouchy manager. "No fucking swears."

"No… well, yes, that too. But more like, do you need a scarf or something?"

"A scarf?" I wrinkled my nose in confusion. It was about a million degrees outside. I was already sweating my balls off in only my T-shirt and jeans.

"Your neck, Dean." Cory blew out an exasperated breath.

"My ne—"

Oh shit. My hand flew to the right side of my neck, under my ear. The spot that Ash had mercilessly exploited since the first time we'd hooked up. The spot where he'd nibbled and sucked in the middle of our third—or was it the fourth?—time last night until I practically came from that contact alone.

Fucking hell. Ash and I were so exhausted and bleary-eyed it was no wonder we had both missed it. He couldn't even put his contacts in this morning because his eyeballs had been rebelling so badly. Recalling how awkward Beau had been, he had probably noticed. And

Christ, I'd told Carter I was hanging out with Ash alone all last night. I couldn't even pass it off as having been with a groupie anymore.

Had they both figured it out?

"How's everybody doing tonight!" Jasmine's voice rang out on stage to thunderous applause.

Panicking, I scanned around the backstage area for a solution as Jasmine pumped up the crowd. I looked at Cory, my eyes wide, begging him to help me in some way. He wouldn't understand why this hickey was different from any other night in the past, but there was no way I could go on stage knowing where the mark had come from.

"Christ, Dean. You okay? It's not that big of a deal. Just, you know, gotta keep a PG image with the charity and the kids. Here," Cory said, pulling off his black hoodie, "take this."

I scowled at the well-worn black Thorns sweatshirt that was several sizes too big.

"And now, please welcome the Inevitable Thorns!" Jasmine yelled into the microphone.

Seeing no better alternative, I threw it on and zipped it up as high as it would go, positioning the hood so it would hopefully hide the evidence. I jogged over to the rest of the guys, who all gave me questioning looks for what I'm sure were different reasons.

The applause grew as the stage lights dimmed.

"You okay?" Ash whispered to me as I grabbed my bass from a stagehand.

"Hickey on my neck," I said as quietly as possible. Ash's eyes went wide and his skin paled.

Carter jumped up and down twice—his standard ritual to psych himself up—before leading the way onto the stage. Ash and I stared at each other, having no choice but to follow.

Ash

THE show went by in a blur. Muscle memory kicked in and I made it through the songs, though I barely remember any of it. My immediate reaction when Dean told me about the hickey was panic. Dean showing up somewhere with scratches or marks on him after a night out was hardly news in the past, even if the thought now made me physically ill. The part that made me anxious was my conversation with Beau as I was getting ready in the dressing rooms, where he'd asked why I hadn't returned his text last night and I mentioned offhandedly that I had been with Dean all evening.

As the show went on, I grew more resigned to what had happened. Beau was smart. He could probably piece the story together. I was planning on telling him and Carter anyway; it just sucked that the whole thing wasn't entirely on my own terms anymore.

"We got one last song for y'all tonight," Carter said into the microphone, addressing the crowd. "It's a new track that I've co-written with Chase Collins, who some of you may remember from our song 'Next to Me.' Anyway, this one is about anyone who's ever felt different or like they don't fit into an older generation's mold. It's called 'Stained Glass Cathedrals and Chantilly Lace.' This crowd's the perfect place to debut it, so I hope you enjoy."

The audience went wild knowing they would hear a new track for the first time. Carter started playing some riffs on his guitar, teasing the song while he let the fans' excitement build. There was nothing like the energy of an appreciative crowd. It wasn't always easy making music for a living, but this was the payoff for all the long days and years spent struggling.

"Oh, and by the way," Carter continued when there was a dip in the applause. "In case you were wondering, Chase and I wrote this the night after we got engaged."

The swell of noise radiating in front of us was insane. The screams and shouts and clapping were more intense than anything I'd ever heard in my life. Holy crap. We didn't know Carter was going to let that little tidbit slip publicly tonight, but it shouldn't have surprised me, with this song debuting. He had come so far over the past eighteen months with how comfortable and self-confident he was. I hoped I would be able to follow his model someday soon.

Without any other buildup or waiting for the uproar to drop, Carter yelled into the mic, "Two, three, four!" And we launched into the new tune.

If the immediate response was any indication, this song was going to be a massive hit. All the energy we were throwing at the crowd was being returned tenfold. I pounded out the tempo on my drums, keeping time and becoming the crowd's collective heartbeat. Beside me was my partner in crime. If I was the heart, Dean was the lungs. Together, we kept the band going with our combined rhythm. Making all the harmonies and beautiful lyrics possible.

Most people think the bass is similar to a regular guitar. In reality, it's closer to the drums. The bass bridges the gap between the melody and the beat. The sound is easy to miss if you're not listening for it, but the bass is the foundation for all the other instruments in a band. Just like Dean is the foundation for the Thorns themselves.

The four-minute song went by like it was only thirty seconds. We wrapped up the show, said our goodbyes to the crowd, and made our way backstage so the crew could take everything apart. Walking with the three other guys, we all experienced the standard postshow high, along with an underlying noticeable tension between us. I glanced around, wanting to make sure we were alone, and nodded at Dean. His eyes went wide, realizing quickly what I wanted to do. He returned my nod almost imperceptibly, supporting me.

"Hey, um, guys?" I said. The four of us stopped walking, and the other Thorns turned to me.

I took Dean's hand in my own for moral support as much as confirmation of what was going on. He squeezed my hand twice in solidarity, meeting my eyes and smiling at me.

"Dean and I are together," I said, letting out a freeing breath. "I'm gay. It wasn't planned, and it hasn't been going on that long, but we want you to know. It's serious, or at least I'm pretty sure it's seri—"

"It is," Dean cut me off. He added his second hand to the pile, sandwiching my right hand with both of his.

Beau rolled his eyes. "It's about fucking time."

"Yeah," Carter added. "We've been waiting for you two to get your heads out of your asses for years."

I choked out an awkward laugh. "Wait, what?"

"I always thought there was more there, didn't you, Cart? They've always been attached at the hip," Beau said.

Carter nodded in agreement. "I definitely wondered about it. But Dean was always such a groupie whore it was hard to know for sure."

"Always came home to Ash, though," Beau noted.

"So you're not surprised?" I asked.

Beau shook his head emphatically.

"Maybe a little," Carter said after a beat. "But it kinda makes perfect sense too."

Dean looked at me and smiled. It was a look that promised everything I'd ever wanted.

"Is this where we start making out in front of them?" Dean asked, alluding to our conversation from the previous night.

I rolled my eyes. No, Dean Phillips would never be the most hopelessly romantic partner in the world, but I couldn't say I minded. He would pick me up an old record he stumbled across in the place of bouquets of roses. We would skip the foamy fish and hundred-dollar bottles of champagne for our burgers and beer. Instead of sexy lingerie, he'd probably be a free-baller for life. All of those things made Dean who he was. Like the song said, we'd form our own traditions. No stained glass cathedrals. No Chantilly lace. Our relationship was unique and perfect in its own way, built on fifteen years of friendship, an ever-increasingly popular catalog of music, and more laughter than I could ever hope for.

That was our bassline. The rhythm of us.

And I never wanted us to change.

Keep Reading for an Excerpt from
Dance with Me
Inevitable Duets, Book #2
by Veronica Cochrane

Beau

"YOU PLAY keyboard most of the time, even when there's a full grand piano on the stage. Why?" Some preppy, glasses-and-button-down-wearing student in the middle asked me with his eyes full of condescension.

I thought about the question for a second, wanting to be honest about my answer but not blatantly insulting to all of the classically trained musicians in the lecture hall. I had agreed to talk to some freshmen as a favor to Chase, a good friend of mine who was an upperclassman in music composition at the Juilliard School. I never liked interviews much to begin with, and I had known going into this thing that my style of playing would be vastly different from what these kids were used to. The students at these types of private conservatories always seemed to have their noses in the air; however, Chase was adamant that the professor wanted to showcase the variety of career paths one could take in the music industry. I respected that, and seeing how Chase was basically the reason I wasn't a washed-up has-been before my twenty-fifth birthday, I was more than amenable to helping out when he approached me. That and I didn't have anything better to do today.

"Um, I guess it just suits me better? I'm not a classical pianist by any stretch of the imagination, and sitting behind a grand doesn't feel right to me most of the time," I answered. "There are a couple songs either Carter or I will play on the piano, but normally the keyboard is a better fit for me and also for our sound."

I was introduced to Chase through his boyfriend, my bandmate Carter West, earlier in the year. When our band, Inevitable Thorns, got back from our first national tour last spring, we struggled to write new music for our sophomore record. The four members of our group shared the songwriting responsibility, but we were all exhausted and were feeling the pressure to create music that lived up to the first release. We were ridiculously lucky that Chase came into our lives and stepped up, cowriting most of the songs that made the final cut. The album was absurdly well received, and our label immediately arranged for us to embark on an eight-month European circuit. A little over two months into the tour, it was going incredibly well, and we were having the time of our lives. However, we still faced some challenges.

Which is why we were here in New York now. Three days between gigs and Carter insisted upon hiring a private plane to fly us all across the Atlantic so he could see his guy. Carter was noticeably smitten with Chase, and fortunately it seemed like Chase was equally infatuated with Carter. It was sweet, really. They were perfect together, and I was exceedingly happy for them, yet seeing them so googly-eyed about each other made me wonder if I was missing out on something.

A couple more hands shot up, but the professor thankfully cut them off before I was forced to answer any more questions.

"I think that's all we have time for today. Thanks so much to Beau Davis for finding an hour in his busy schedule to join us. Class, remember your midterm paper is due in two weeks. Do *not* leave this one to the last minute."

The students shuffled—putting away notebooks and laptops, chatting with their neighbors as they left. I stuck around, and the professor and I made small talk for a minute or two. He began to pack up his things, so I thanked him again and headed for the exit. As I entered the adjoining hallway, I looked out the windows to see that it was absolutely pissing down rain outside. When Chase had walked me in, we'd entered through a hidden door in the courtyard that was right next to the classroom. Chase had already finished his classes and left, taking advantage of the few hours he had remaining with Carter.

I decided to cut through a hallway that looked like it led in the opposite direction, attempting to exit the building closer to the street, where I could hopefully catch a cab. The corridors had emptied quickly; it was getting late, and I figured most of the students were probably done for the day.

I made my way through the empty corridor for a while before realizing it curved around on itself and didn't appear to have an external door. Hearing music from the end of the hall, I decided to keep going in the hopes that someone could point me in the right direction. As I grew closer, I realized that it wasn't just any song that was playing, but one of Thorns's songs—the only one that I had written for our new album.

Before Chase had become involved, we only had a couple of usable tunes, one of which I had penned. The song was titled "Galaxies," and though it wasn't the most recognizable track on the sophomore record, it was meaningful to me, and our hard-core fans still knew the words by heart. When we played it in large theaters and stadiums, we encouraged the audience to shine the flashlights on their phones up at the stage. The vast auditoriums looked like they were filled with stars, and it was always a beautiful moment in the show.

I poked my nose into the room where the music was coming from, and my breath caught in my throat. A lone dancer flew through the air, graceful and perfectly in sync with the lyrics Carter sang. Reacting physically, I leaned in closer, completely in awe of the scene in front of me.

The dance studio itself was unassuming. A row of full-length mirrors covered one wall, with ballet barres lining the others, except for some space next to the door where there were shelves for students to store their things. A couple of posters above the shelves featured ballerinas in pointe shoes, with motivational sayings. The floor was black, and the ceiling was lofty, with speakers embedded high in the corners so you could hear the music from wherever you happened to be.

The dancer was breathtaking. He wore next to nothing—a simple pair of nude boy shorts that left very little to the imagination—but surprisingly his outfit wasn't what captured my attention. The lines of his body were so fluid as he progressed through the dance. His movements were impossibly complex. Yet he made them look effortless. He was wild but controlled. Purposeful, though animalistic. Graceful and masculine. A jumble of contradictions that fought logic and gender norms in a beautiful display of dynamism. The power he radiated from every muscle and tendon was paralyzing.

The dancer's core was a perfect six-pack. His body was sculpted by practical use, not only for show, chiseled out of exercising for a living instead of hours spent ballooning at the gym. His legs extended each time he jumped; even his toes were stretching and pointing. His arms were long and elegant, holding tension and shifting around an invisible partner.

The piece was a duet. I could see that now from his movements. The passion he conveyed in every motion, every *breath*, was a fervent expression of desire. I had never been particularly enthusiastic about staged dance routines—they had always seemed dry and pompous to me, much like playing the piano instead of the keyboard—but the way this man showcased his body to a rock song shattered every preconception in my mind.

And it was *sexy*.

My God, the strength needed to lift and move himself so effortlessly captured my focus to the point that I didn't even notice when the music faded away and the song ended.

The dancer bent over and rested his hands on his knees. His chest rose and fell quickly as he fought to catch his breath from the vigorous feat. After a moment he stood and ran his fingers through his hair, drawing my attention to it. Despite his exertion the dancer's hair was still perfectly coiffed. It was the most beautiful color of mahogany red, longer on the top than the sides in a pompadour style. His locks were complemented by a well-maintained short beard that I had the immediate desire to feel scraping across my skin.

I shuddered involuntarily at the thought.

As he was already covered in a light sheen of sweat, it didn't take much to slot this man into the fantasy category. His intense blue eyes flickered up in the mirror, sensing my presence and, embarrassingly, noticing me drooling over him. Despite the feeling of being caught with my hand in the cookie jar, I couldn't force myself to look away. A crease furrowed his brow as he turned to face me, replaced a second later by a look of recognition.

"Holy shit, you're Beau Davis," he told me.

While I had grown somewhat accustomed to being recognized in public, it was never as frequent for me as it was for Carter, or when I was out with a second band member. It still threw me off a little when it happened. It was weird that people knew who I was. With overly enthusiastic fans, I had a hard time deciding exactly how I should react. In general, I mostly kept to myself, preferring to relax with a book or a movie after a concert instead of tracking down parties and groupies with my bandmate Dean.

"I am." I chuckled out loud at his assessment. "Sorry for barging in. I got lost and heard music down the hall. That was… wow… that was amazing," I said, struggling to adequately express how moved I was by what I had seen.

His blue eyes sparkled, and he grinned at me. He moved closer to the doorframe I had somehow become glued to.

"Thank you. It's still a work in progress. Obviously. But that's so cool you liked it. I'm Jamie, by the way." He extended his hand for a shake.

It was such a simple gesture—the smallest, most mundane amount of contact. Nonetheless, feeling his skin for the first time gave me butterflies. His hands were smooth and soft, unlike my own calloused musician's hands. I caught myself staring at our joined hands, feeling a little slow because of his touch.

"Oh, sorry," he said, looking down at the expanse of his bare chest, likely assuming that was what I was gaping at.

Now that he'd drawn my attention to it, I couldn't take my eyes off his torso. Jamie plucked a T-shirt off of the floor and pulled it over his head at leisure, seemingly unbothered by his own nakedness. I looked up to meet his gaze, pretending I hadn't been ogling him.

"So what are you doing here at Juilliard?" He asked.

I forced myself out of my stupor, trying to focus and be a coherent conversationalist.

"Oh, um, I was a guest at one of the first-year music classes. A favor to a friend of mine," I replied, still feeling sluggish and stupidly affected by this stranger in front of me.

"Cool. The students must have loved having you," he said, smile easy and warm.

"I dunno about that." I laughed. "I think I'm a little too rough around the edges for the Juilliard crowd."

"Some of us like it rough." He winked at me.

My face got hot from his blatant flirting; I had no idea how to respond. No way did he know how accurate that statement was. Right?

"But seriously," Jamie continued, smirking at my flustered reaction, "they need a shake-up when they first get here. They're always too classical. Too focused on the rules. Nothing great comes out of simply copying what someone else does."

The unexpected profoundness of Jamie's statement affected me. I had never been formally trained or had aspirations to be any type of prim and proper musician.

Not that there was anything wrong with that; it just wasn't who I was or a part of the opportunities I had been given in life. Ever since I'd walked into the building earlier, I had felt *less than*. Less than trained. Less than classy. Less than part of the elite—which was ridiculous, because I made more money and had more fans than I knew what to do with. Yet I couldn't help but think back to a time when that hadn't been the case.

It had been a weird day all around.

"Hey, so I'm sure you've got stuff to do, and you probably get this all the time, but any chance I can buy you a drink and ask you a few questions about your music?" Jamie asked. "There's a couple bits of this piece I'm struggling with, and it would be amazing to get your opinion." He ran a towel over his face and began throwing his stuff into a bag.

Something about Jamie was calling out to me. Obviously he was gorgeous, but I was drawn to him for other reasons I couldn't fully describe. I had no idea why I was so fascinated by him. All I knew was there was no way I was going to pass up a chance to spend more time in the company of this captivating man.

"I'm not much of a dancer. Not sure I'd be any help." I smiled self-consciously. "But yeah, I've got some time."

Jamie

"YOU DIDN'T!" Beau exclaimed, laughing uninhibitedly over the top of his second beer.

"Totally did. So after I came offstage, the costume designer and the director called me over and chewed my ass off about the changes I made to my outfit. They *did* stop short of firing me on the spot—probably because they didn't want to teach someone else the part overnight. But the review in the *Times* the next day specifically raved about how my outfit was the perfect dramatic paradox—that's what they said: "dramatic paradox"—for the piece. Long, *long* story short, that plus an injury made me decide that telling people what to do is way better than being told. Creating my own shit is more fun than dancing the stuffy old *Nutcracker* every year for eternity."

"So you became a choreographer," Beau concluded.

"So I became a choreographer." I nodded. "And now those pretentious pricks keep me employed because I do my job well and they're terrified of me leaving to go work for another company. Plus they take care of the boring admin crap like getting the licensing rights to use the music, so I can't complain too much."

I paused to take a sip of my drink. "Ballet isn't just classical pieces anymore. It can be modern. Lyrical. Emotional and exciting. Contemporary dance is every bit as important as the *Swan Lakes* of the world. It makes people feel and connect. Sometimes it's easier to express yourself and tell a story with movement instead of words."

Yes, I was aware I probably sounded cocky as fuck to the Grammy-winning, world-class musician sitting beside me on his bar stool, but I couldn't help it. Talking about dance—especially my type of dance—brought out the passion in me, and it was hard to remember to tone it down when I got on a roll.

"Wow, that's amazing. Now that you mention it, I vaguely remember going through the music rights for stuff like that with our agent. Guess I hadn't really thought about it. I had no idea people actually do, like, choreography to Thorns's songs. Dancing at a club or something, yeah. But what you did in there? That was something else." Beau's soulful brown eyes were wide.

Tonight was a trip. I had no idea how I'd ended the night in my local bar talking to this crazy-talented man. Inevitable Thorns was one of my all-time favorite bands. I had choreographed to a couple of their pieces over the years. Their music seemed to lend itself perfectly to the way I liked to create movement: fluid, with an intensity behind it. Melodic but filled with edge and angst. The Thorns songs were filled with stories of love and tragedy, more akin to opera than a lot of the crap on the radio today.

The piece I had been working on earlier was one of the lesser-known songs on their latest album. That was another thing I loved—not sticking to the single or the obvious choice for the music. It was like bringing new life to a piece that might be forgotten over time. "Galaxies" was just as deserving of accolades as any of Thorns's bigger hits, but there were simply too many good tracks in their catalog for all of them to become sensations.

"I'm really happy you liked it. Like I said, it's still a work in progress."

I raised my glass to my lips to take a gulp of the cool liquid.

"Can I ask you something?" I asked, not wanting to squander the opportunity to talk to Beau about his music. He nodded and gestured for me to go on. "So I guess I'm just trying to figure out how to play the ending. It's so ambiguous in the final verse. I know that he leaves his lover because of the hurt she's caused, but there's still hope there too. Does that mean she eventually gets better? Do they find their way back to each other?"

He smiled at me, seemingly enjoying listening to my interpretation of the lyrics his band had written.

"What?" I finally asked. I furrowed my brow, self-consciousness getting the best of me. "I'm not that far off, am I?"

"No, not far off." Beau stroked his chin before continuing slowly. "I guess I don't really know about the ending. I did need to leave to get out of a bad situation, but I'm always optimistic that the other person will eventually find their way. Not so we can be together. For themself. So it *is* kind of ambiguous, in my mind at least. The listener can interpret it as either cautiously hopeful for the future or the end of the relationship."

I thought for a moment about that unhelpful comment. Vagueness wasn't the worst thing in the world, but I wished Beau had a clearer answer. There was something about the piece that called out to me. I got the sense that I was circling the spark, the magic. It seemed to be just outside my grasp, but I couldn't put my finger on what exactly *it* was.

"But, um… it's not about a she," Beau added quietly. "At least it wasn't when I wrote it."

I paused for a second, genuinely caught off guard.

"Oh shit, seriously?" I asked. "You're gay?"

"Bi, actually. But this song was about a guy. I didn't, like, purposely leave out pronouns or anything, they just didn't work into the lyrics. I kinda liked how it turned out, not weighed down by answers or concrete details. Or gender. It's not a song that gets talked about much, so nobody's really asked us during interviews or anything."

Egoistically I was far more engrossed by the new ideas this admission generated for my choreography than about Beau's personal confession. Even before I consciously thought it through, I knew immediately that this was the flame I had been looking for. My head was spinning.

The piece I had been creating was a typical duet between a man and a woman. I had already mentally cast the male lead, but I was having a hard time deciding who the female should be. This revelation offered the opportunity to change things.

I suddenly felt alive with possibility. My blood pumped rapidly through my body, thumping loudly in my ears. The skin on my arms grew tight with goose bumps, and my whole body vibrated with the creative energy that was flowing. Now that the idea was embedded, I couldn't picture the number as a traditional male/female pas de deux anymore.

It needed to be danced by two men.

Fuck.

It *needed* to be danced by two men.

DREAMSPUN DESIRES

Now Available
Dance with Me

by Veronica Cochrane
An Inevitable Duets Romance

When dance instructor Jamie Griffin choreographs a contemporary ballet pas de deux to a love song by rock band Inevitable Thorns, he doesn't expect the band's keyboardist, Beau Davis, to witness it. He definitely doesn't expect the steamy one-night stand that follows.

Beau leaves to continue touring, but he can't get Jamie or his passion out of his head... especially once a video of the dance goes viral. This leads to a chance for the two of them to reconnect on tour, with Jamie performing his dance while the band plays live. The lines between a casual fling and a forever romance blur as rock music and ballet join to create magic onstage.

That magic suffuses their relationship too, but the price of fame is steep. When an explosive interview threatens the foundation of what they're building together, will Beau and Jamie set the record straight and define their relationship—and their art—on their own terms? Or will the stars they're reaching for elude their grasp?